Personal Effects

Personal Effects

Carmel Macdonald Grahame

UWA PUBLISHING

First published in 2014 by
UWA Publishing
Crawley, Western Australia 6009
www.uwap.uwa.edu.au

UWAP is an imprint of UWA Publishing,
a division of The University of Western Australia.

A full CIP entry is available from the National Library of Australia.

Typeset in Bembo by Lasertype
Printed by Lightning Source

This project has been assisted by the Australian Government
through the Australia Council for the Arts, its arts funding and advisory body.

For David

One

Living is moving; time is a live creek bearing changing lights. As I move, or as the world moves around me, the fullness of what I see shatters – Annie Dillard

No matter how easily I use it to name my relationship with Ross I have never been comfortable with the word *wife* to describe my occupation, but here we go again. Little else feels familiar about being back here in Calgary, Alberta, Canada.

Not for us a suburban vista this time. Outside, the untidy three dimensions of the downtown core are being licked by snow. A crane's boom slides across the sky and disappears into the flurry. A cityscape silently enveloped while I watch, and a delivery of beauty that depends on silence, is nothing like the windy storms I am used to, where noisy rain-dimpled ocean thrashes white sand.

Which could explain why snow seems to represent some quintessential otherness just now, has me feeling my strangerhood keenly and as if some kind of nomadism were always unfolding in me. Cervantes. Calgary. Places on opposite sides of a world. There can't be many in whose lives they meet. I feel like a stitch binding them together, a stitch in place.

Being here at all means Ross and I are passing across our own footsteps, the way my reflected image passes back and forth across the snow-filled windows. It is an image increasingly interrupted and disjointed as I unpack, by accumulating reflections of books, notebooks, various totems to make us feel at home (photographs, a row of mosaic bowls, the ferocious features of a Barong painting bought in Bali years ago), a vase of purple tulips, the blue back of my laptop (I must remember to call it a notebook here), and now a bell-shaped glass standing companionably beside the bottle of wine I have just opened.

I consider the last, knowing I am not immune. Loneliness could have me slipping down that throat that goes on swallowing people whole, swallowing whole people. Only I refuse to become any such cliché, so far at least, the exercise of small disciplines being how I have learned to invent a life out of each new place.

This collection of images is the present tense, I tell myself, that woman in the window. The now, the here. *Get used to it*, I instruct her. In the background float too many boxes she has yet to unpack. Tomorrow.

Is her birthday.

Reflected in the window this lit-up room is an aquarium. I, floating in it, am a fishwife. The stack of boxes looms behind me like a container ship emerging out of fog. It is still surprising how displeased I was by their arrival. As men manoeuvred it all through the door and the room became less and less empty, I discovered I like to have empty space around me.

Stuff, I think now. Boxes crammed with home, there, then, detritus from the immediate and far past mocking my discipline and organisation at the other end. All that storing, donating, abandoning, all that paring down of our lives to what we would need to stand up in. The boxes strike me as unfriendly guests to whom I have an obligation, have their hands on their hips, spoil the sense of air, light, newness, spaciousness that had begun making me feel as if life had been lanced, the feeling that comes with starting again.

Not that starting again is ever an uncomplicated pleasure, and this time the excitement of transplantation is wearing off quickly. Ross leaving so soon has siphoned away my sense of adventure, turning it into a particular blend of anticipation and worry. He could be flying the two hundred or more kilometres from St John's to a rig in the North Atlantic at this very minute. Out there helicopters ferry workers back and forth, depositing them in rotating batches so the rig can work on and on, draining the earth of oil.

I am mindful that every few years Ross is required to upgrade his training in how to escape from a drowning helicopter, and each time the dreadful possibilities enter my head. He makes jokes about the Jesus bolt, so-called because it connects a helicopter to its rotor blades and hence everything depends on it. I refuse to find them funny.

Once again I will do the settling in, with no distractions this time but to gaze down on the heads of countless strangers going about their lives. The city's vital signs: Stetsons, cowboy boots sticking out like oars, the broad shoulders of heavy overcoats, occasionally made of luxuriant fur. Fifteen storeys float between me and that street, and a sudden unwelcome desire to measure the fall tells me I have begun sounding the depths of disappointment, need to remind myself not to become that tight-lipped woman again. The thick hush of living so high above the traffic has me in danger of self-pity, home tugging at my heart.

Cervantes clings to the Turquoise Coast of Western Australia. When I grew up there, looking it up on a dubdubdub dot was inconceivable, but now it exists as this small string of words I summon to my computer screen: 'Cervantes: 245 miles north of Perth. Shire: Dandaragan. Pop. 532. Postcode: 6511.' Whoever made the entry was still thinking in miles. At this distance the anachronism seems appropriate.

Few people here could relate to our harsh landscape, or the plants of the kwongan – acacias and banksias with their serrated edges, star-sharp austerity, their spikes, the stiff nutty conglomerations clustering on sticks and branches, the galactic flowers New Holland honeyeaters and honey possums find irresistible. The whole area honeyed, honeying, and beekeepers out there harvesting flavours from the buzz and hum of the bush. Place of grasses, heath, space.

I leave the computer to its planetary screensaver, pick up one of my mosaic bowls, move it closer to its partners on the unfamiliar shelves – the fiddling of housewifery, tiny attentions to the positions of objects and relationships between them, size, colour, shape, function, the constantly straying and rearranging hands of the homemaker. The bowl seems heavier than I remember. Not least, I am aware, with time passed since I lined its belly with yellow porcelain chips and the tiny gold clay tiles that seem awkwardly made now, a clumsy *pique assiette* effect I would resist these days. But I could never part with this work, over which I bled, literally – and I use that word advisedly – which could be why I decided on the particular bowls to bring with me this time. This one seems suddenly big in my hand, and odd that it should be here, can actually have arrived in this far-removed room.

Pique assiette, I am reminded, derives from *piquer*, to prick, or irritate, and can mean 'stolen plate' in French, because the eccentric Raymond Isidore who made the process famous in the first half of the twentieth century begged, borrowed and stole china to paste onto the surfaces of his Chartres home. His neighbours thought him mad and his house ridiculous and pronounced him a *picassiette*, abusively, but I like to think Raymond Isidore was able to ignore their unneighbourly appraisals of his compulsion. He was posthumously vindicated as an artist, since the mosaic genre is named after him, and the house, now called La Maison Picassiette, is a popular destination among aficionados of the mosaic arts.

Ross and I visited there one Sunday morning, only to find it closed. Heavy rain and a high dense hedge on which I scratched my cheek trying – I still have that scar too – made it impossible to see, but I was temperate about disappointment by that time, which real loss had already taught me I eventually take in my stride. I was probably preoccupied with memories of having travelled from Australia to Agra years earlier to see the Taj Mahal in moonlight and failing, that time because of cloud cover.

There is no stopping cloud. Nor the concertina of connections the mind will make at a given moment, a thought that strikes me as appropriate, given how *pique assiette* mosaics are called memory ware. These memories of Chartres bring with them sudden insight into how unsuccessful my more deliberate pilgrimages have been. Life has gone best when I was wandering cooperatively along the lines of whatever map happened to be unfurling under me. I must do that this time, cooperate with circumstances, submit.

Ross and I retreated from the wet Chartres hedge to the cathedral, where I knelt on stones that once bore the weight of Joan of Arc. It seemed like an awesome substitution and was adequate compensation to a woman from Cervantes with a penchant for significance. I try to remember the small lessons, carry them with me, keep in mind how each place inhabits you, makes its way forward with you into the present tense.

Replacing the bowl at a more precise distance from its companions I consider attachments to things, questions of sentimental value, think about how unexpectedly loss and damage can flower. *Pique assiette* mosaics, for example, are a mode of recomposition. Like fabric applied to a quilt, pieces of a grandmother's broken cup, say, can be arranged and rearranged, each bringing its particular accidental shape to the whole and determining form. You take damage and convert it into something that will differently endure. You take what is old and preserve it. You revel in disparity as much as harmony. You transform, reconfigure, complete. You line pieces up and follow their flow. Any multiplicity of wholes can be dismantled and their parts differently fused. You take the past and send it, refashioned, into the future.

All of which I have done for so long I suspect I think in pieces. Easy enough when you take your cues from a past smashed to smithereens.

All this introspection is more than my usual managed sense of Ross's absence. I am used to missing him, having accepted long ago that we exist in overlapping lives – his, ours, mine, usually in that order. Somewhere along the way I learned to imagine my way into the Ross-only strands, am aware that in their recent history lie the origins of my latest displacement and the various reasons for this mood that has me crouching over notions of what life could have been like had I been the one doing so much of the leaving.

The poorer, certainly.

This time, I decide, I will make a friend of the woman in the window. She can keep me company, teach me to stand the embalming cold again. She and I both know she is not the only phantom I watch for in this freezing city.

If she were real, perhaps we would be curled up on the new, self-indulgently cream linen sofa discussing how a feature of any good marriage is what John Keats apparently described as 'one of the most mysterious of semi-speculations…that of one Mind's imagining into another'. I might be thinking aloud about how I fancy Ross and I are still socketed into each other's lives because we share the gift of being able to imagine our way in. Perhaps I would be trying to explain how I come to be back here in Calgary, and she might be willing, as a friend would be, to listen.

As it is, I cannot remember the last time I enjoyed curled-up, girl-talk intimacy with another woman. I turn to my journals. Or, as now, murmur occasionally to myself, this time in a muffled apartment, my thoughts constantly returning to my absent husband. The speculations I fancy Keats was talking about are how I make sense of the fact that I am standing in this particular place watching a city disappear into winter.

Then I give melodrama the flick.

Just weeks earlier and a desert storm has come and gone. The flood that followed is draining down channel country. The sodden Queensland desert is hatching insects by the millions. The rig lights attract them. This particular night, countless moths are incinerating themselves against massive wattage, and a nauseating smell of burning pervades the place.

The earth outside Ross's donga is soft with the feathery, dusty dead – big brown buggers with black false eyes on their wings. Over the whole camp, thousands, and over the desert – he couldn't imagine it really – must be billions. The beetles are the worst. Crunching across the teeming ground, he can feel his weight killing them with every step and there is no way of avoiding it. With the humidity as the soaking earth dries out, the conditions are the like of which he has never felt, not even in Dubai, where it was hotter but hadn't rained for a year when he was last there, a circumstance that seems preferable to working all day in saturated 48-degree heat like this.

Over the last week Ross has learned to whip the accommodation module door open and closed, but no matter how hard he tries the air conditioner is clogging up with moths, crickets and beetles that make their way in with him. Right now he is exhausted, and clogged or not a clunking air conditioner means the room is cooler than the outside air, so he slams the door shut behind him, hoping for a decent night's sleep.

After he's got started on this report, this bloody final report that will mean they want to shoot the messenger: him.

He wakes next morning to dead insects among the bedclothes, even in the folds of his pyjamas. The carapace of a huge beetle has left scratches on his belly. He swears at the walls.

Outside, heat presses up at him again. He is walking on steam. The floods are still subsiding and where they have ebbed away the land is left puffing.

Instructions on the backs of toilet doors remind everyone to drink six litres of water a day and announce the enforcement of the buddy system. The men must watch each other for signs of dehydration: vagueness, disorientation – nothing could be more dangerous on a rig floor than losing concentration or consciousness. Equipment will wind itself around parts of a man's body and lop them off quick as look at you; a drill pipe left to its own devices will flip him out of existence.

Walking to the showers is the usual nightmare, and in some respects a waste of time, because on the way back the mud-sponge underfoot only dirties you up again, and the humidity has you sweating again, and the bugs you brush off leave pieces of themselves behind. But it is an indescribable pleasure to have cool water running over his skin, unslicking him, and his hands lathering soap over his body return him to it comfortably for this few minutes at least, making him think of Lilith and home, where by contrast his body is indulged, nurtured, sustained, where his sense of his own humanity is retooled, where there is the dependable return to how he believes human beings are meant to feel – comfortable, well-tuned, loved.

Every time you went through this kind of physical strain — kept working no matter the heat, cold, or any other duress — you knew love and learned to value it. At least he did. And he would soon be back there, back to normal, which seems more like a place than a condition just now. Normal: it has physical dimensions and entry and exit points. It begins at his and Lilith's front door... wherever that may end up being when this is over.

Ross has hoped against hope to be leaving in the morning, but the Land Rovers will leave for the airstrip before five and there is no way men going out on shift change will risk missing a flight, especially for an outsider like him. If he doesn't finish up today, and he won't, he'll be stuck for another week.

He can hear the disappointment in Lilith's voice.

'So what's the problem this time?'

'They reckon the well's drying up, but I can't see it. Something else is going on. It'll be money, of course. It's been a stinker of a job from the start. Look, I'll be out of here as soon as I can, Lili, but it'll be next week.'

True to form she cheers him up with a description of strawberries meticulously applied to a garden bench she's doing up for someone in the hills. Ross knows the quality of his wife's work — better than she does, he suspects. The result is probably some gorgeous representation of abundance, a cornucopia laid out for the eye to relish. She's been getting more and more commissions lately, and better and better at them.

'Too precious for words,' she's saying, 'but paid work, and you know how I feel about that...'

'Anything for a dollar?' An old joke between them.

'Clearly.'

Ross is watching a dingo family, mates and a pup, hanging around on the edge of camp, thin, rangy creatures that have come in out of the desert night, eating insects, snapping hopefully up towards the bright lights of the hi-tech oasis. From early in their marriage he and Lilith have made it a habit to describe to each other what they are looking at when talking on the phone like this, so he tries to summon up the way the dingoes are melting along the lines of a shed, the watchfulness that is evident even at this distance.

After they hang up – You. No You. No, your turn... still, after all these years, a private well-worn routine and how he knows she has reached the point of really missing him – Ross sits for a minute watching the dingoes led even further in by moths they stir up as they run, snapping and biting at the air, feeding on the fluttering brown cloud rising in front of them. The animals slink and cringe at the edges of the light, pretending to be invisible, but they come on in nonetheless.

Poor bastards – drought–flood cycle, hard to imagine how they've survived. Either there was high ground somewhere out there or they've come a bloody long way – probably been on the run for days. *They'd have to be incredibly hungry to do it*, Ross thinks. And that hunger shouldn't be taken lightly, either, not lightly at all, not after the awful stuff that happened to the Chamberlains, and others since. *Dingoes are shy wild creatures and their best friends we are not*, Ross thinks, walking to his room.

Another week to go, then back to Perth. And then it's over and done with, possibly even his career. He thinks the word with a mental grimace. It might turn out to be just as well Lilith isn't anchored to a job. The only decent work he's hearing about is in Canada and the Middle East. The question is not whether he can ask her to go through all that again, but whether at their age they have a choice.

The day he got back there was no need to ask. Fatigue was written all over him.

'Sorry,' he said kissing me a tired abrasive kiss. 'It was shave or catch the plane. I caught the plane.'

'Burke and Wills country?'

'Yeah, I saw the memorial. How they imagined they'd get through out there without dying…It must have taken courage, but you have to wonder about their lack of humility as well. God, I'm glad to be home. You have no idea…'

'Good,' I said, knowing he was right.

Later, showered, shaved and slumped in the window armchair, ice clinking in a rum and Coke, he told me about a deluge of insects, among other things, working his way up to confiding that as soon as the job was finished we would need to make tough decisions.

'We have to face facts.' He came out with it eventually. 'Our best options won't be in Australia, yet again.'

Ours. Ross was always generous with that small word.

All this is how I come to find myself watching a snowstorm while trying to envisage an insect plague and my new, unpredictable future in the same breath, seeming to have entwined the two in my imagination. Distorting both, no doubt, which begins to show now I am here unpacking a shipment in fits and starts in a place that broods with times even further past, even more difficult to hang onto, or imagine.

The thing is everything that happens, happens *somewhere*, a self-evident fact that strikes me as significant and overlooked. Memories insist on staging themselves, so events, moments, periods of a life come back with their mise en scène. Yes, mise en scène – let me not pretend I've learned less than I have about ways of seeing the world.

Hence out of my Cervantes girlhood a vague gazebo floats. There are fences, trees, paddocks. A corner of verandah juts out, from which on a clear day you used to be able to glimpse the sea. A scrawny rose garden perseveres despite salt winds and sometimes desperate heat. Bush tracks wind off into banksia forests beyond which there are a Painted Desert, a Pudding Hill, a Kangaroo Point and Hangover Bay, which – family joke – we used to say my father must have been responsible for naming. Cray boats still bob on the sea there. Dolphins still flirt with you when you spend time on the jetty. In the background of any act of remembering are the places, mirage-like, holding events together, as potent as cathedrals, mind-henges.

I expect these ruminations are an effect of age making me as intrigued by questions of place as time, by how some places accrete like mother-of-pearl, hang onto the memory, become heavy, nacreous, sometimes sharp-edged, so it can hurt a little carrying them around – although I believe everything worthwhile comes of the effort. This fact is a key to my retrospections.

Another is the converse reality that life's big events happen anyway, no matter where you are, won't wait for you to feel at home, safe and cosseted. Things can go right anywhere. And wrong.

So I can imagine Ross looking at his watch. One thirty, say. Outside, the Swan River would be sparkling, wind up. Perhaps he expects to see the usual windsurfers scudding between Perth and South Perth like bright-winged insects, the ferry plodding back and forth from Barrack Street, shags shrugging their round shoulders along the river wall.

If he takes a lunch break before the wrap-up he could get in a quick walk by going along Riverside Drive and cutting back at the Causeway. Even if it isn't the day out there he's hoping for, it's got to be better than the sweatbox conditions he's spent the last couple of weeks in, although he'd take that over this arid office atmosphere any day. When you spend most of your life in them, fluorescence-filled air-conditioned buildings can seem like a version of hell. Right now he'd give anything to be blown about in real daylight for half an hour, humidity notwithstanding.

Switching off his machine and stretching, he is reminded of his wife's advice to do this every twenty minutes, but the last hour and a half has passed without him even looking up. Like everyone else here, his mind has been chained to a computer screen well into afternoon. *Lilith's right, it is a kind of enslavement*, he thinks, looking over the mezzanine railing into the pool of workers below. Green glass anthill: floor upon floor of blandness, bleakness, people engaged in repetitive sitting, standing, walking rituals to remind their bodies they are capable of sitting, standing, walking. Something has been lost, he decides. Heat, salt, insects seem absolutely more decent than all this day in, day out. He grabs his jacket.

For the past eighteen months, whenever he's in town, Ross has occupied an office next to one Walter Reeves, who writes jokes and sticks them beneath a poster-sized photograph of an obese woman. She is naked with a paper bag over her head in some awful parody of Ned Kelly. The Wally, as even his mates call him, changes the jokes regularly. Passing his desk this day, Ross notices that the latest has to do with decapitation.

A matter of inspiration, Walter insists. He believes he's hilarious and tells anyone who'll listen that in another life he would have been a writer of jokes, a stand-up comic, but that there's no money in art these days.

'Never has been,' Ross replies pretty much each time, Lilith's defence-of-the-realm speeches always springing to mind, but Walter only shrugs, assuming he knows all there is to know about The Arts, making him a man with more options than most in the mining game.

This time Ross passes the unfortunate pinned-up woman with a deep sense of relief that it'll be one of the last. Photography is at the top of a list of things *he* might have done in another life, could still do, which may explain why this so offends him. Whenever his thoughts travel down this road Ross thinks of the triumvirate, the word being a mental genuflection to his family – he wouldn't have swapped life with Lilith and the two girls for anything, certainly not any career thing. He can even summon up a smidgen of feeling for Walter, whose wife is in the process of leaving him, it seems. Although who can blame her. *But poor bastard*, Ross thinks. Perhaps the man isn't bad, just misguided.

Making his way downstairs, Ross wonders about being so misguided himself that he could ever have set his sights on this as a way to spend his life, remembers when the prospect of working here seemed cutting-edge, hi-tech, competitive, the place to be if you wanted to make it. That naïve kid is not so lightly dismissed, either, shadows him on the escalator, triggers another memory further back, of being an undergraduate working on a professor's research project and discovering a downside to having a flair for research. *There has turned out to be a downside to absolutely everything*, he reflects, a fact you'd think he'd be used to by now.

They were measuring the effects of salt levels on the soil down around Lake Grace. Was that it? Christ, *there* was a battle lost. He remembers waking up in a pup tent on the dry lake to a sound like rustling tissue. At first he could see only the white flats glowing in moonlight, but then the surface appeared to be moving and turned out to be alive with white spiders, smooth-bodied, thick-legged creatures, of which far too many seemed to be scurrying around. Next morning he could find no sign, no webs or trapdoors. He thought he must have dreamt it – although it seemed real enough for him to make sure the tent was thoroughly sealed next night, and when the same thing happened he was bloody glad to be sleeping on that raised cot. So many arachnids, small and ethereal-looking though they may be and probably harmless, could make even his spine tingle. After that he was restless every night there, half-expecting to be borne away while he slept.

Maybe it was then that the idea of office work entered his bloodstream. He'd always been interested in the main game, it was true, and security began hanging about in the front of his mind once he became a father. Whatever the reasons, he never pursued geology in the field, and right now it strikes him as regrettable.

Ross shakes off these thoughts, knows he is exactly where he placed himself, that it is nonsense to see his job as some kind of incarceration, but the idea of a tent pitched on a salt lake surface bubbling with white spiders going about their moonlit business has him shaking his head. Cool night air, nothing like it. The bush, solitude, work that really goes somewhere, means something – he just can't seem to rid himself of this heavy sense of having taken a wrong turn, has never felt so disenchanted.

He should have bought those bloody Poseidon shares all those years ago. Well of course he should have; if the beginnings had been that different, who knows what options he and Lilith might be facing now?

Plunging into the wind tunnel that is St Georges Terrace, Ross goes on fending off thoughts of being stuck in a sedentary, radioactive life and expected to be grateful for it. In his game you are measured at some point in ways that go against your own interests. He knows it from watching other men and suspects the point is hereabouts for him. Age. A few blokes even resort to hair dye.

And contracts die for a lot of reasons. This time the simple fact that a well could be drying up would at least be a half-decent reason for laying people off in an industry where decency increasingly has subdued value. But big dollars are in the mix, as always, and the usual bullies and cowboys are treating people more and more contemptibly, although it hardly matters at this stage.

He buys Chinese takeaway for lunch, asks for mono-free, takes it as good advice when the slip of paper in today's fortune cookie reads: 'If you want life to be plain sailing, don't get the wind up.'

Later he can only shake his head when a man who hasn't even bothered to change out of gym gear flicks a two-dollar coin across a conference table and says to someone Ross happens to know has twice the experience and has been on the verge of letting this project cost him his family, 'There! That's what your contribution's been worth, mate.'

Then he walks out, saying over his shoulder, 'Deal's done.'

In the quiet that follows it feels like they sit listening to the sound of each other's lives ticking away. So that's what it's been about. He was right. The well hasn't dried up. Things are being set up to move the work offshore. Cheaper labour. They're determined to make it look as if they have good reasons for it, that's all.

Eventually Walter laughs into the heavy pause, summing up. 'This whole fucking job has been a totally class act,' he says to no one in particular. For once they all agree with him.

By the end of the day Ross can't wait to leave the building. It's a kind of claustrophobic panic. With the revolving door spinning behind him, finally, he can think of a million reasons why he ought to be delighted to be turning his back on it all, but knows it won't be easy. This is not the first time he's had no control over what happens next, but it's the first time he can remember knowing that what he feels about it is a kind of fear.

A few days later Ross breaks a long, dozy driving silence on the way to Cervantes: 'Nearly home.'

'Hmm, home.'

The word has begun to bounce: place where one lives permanently, as a member of a family or household. I am soon chasing what it might mean to us in a month's time, or two; how even if we can never think again in terms of permanence, home will always be here. The sources of my restlessness are here, in the eloquent wind, folded into childhood hours spent on a verandah looking out over paddocks, or standing on beaches looking out to sea and coming up smack against the horizon. I grew up watching suns sink here, wishing, not knowing for what most of the time, except it had to do with being elsewhere and at the same time never leaving.

My father had a small spread twenty minutes' drive north-east of town – mine being a family in which farms are called spreads, although all that is well in the past and we became suburban beings long ago. Other branches of the family still have spreads scattered from here to way down south: Kojonup, Katanning, Albany, Esperance. At least, they live in the farming areas that sprawl around those big country centres like ocean currents – the Great Southern, Plantagenet. Western Australia's shires are huge and throughout them, in small towns that sprouted wherever trains stopped to pick up wheat, houses are bunched around a main street with a post office, a pub, a couple of shops, a school if you're lucky. Many of them are dying now, but isn't everything?

With Cervantes the attraction was always the sea. The town exists because of cray fishing, clutches the coast with small dry claws, its face set against salt winds that hassle the fleet, which is why more than twenty minutes inland a farmer feels salt in the wind and my father's was only ever a small spread and life disappointed him.

This day, Ross and I head down to the beach first, as usual. The sand is heavy underfoot. Passing the tourist board depicting a three-masted ship in full sail, I distract myself from the physical effort with rote facts like the *Cervantes* hit a reef here on 29 June 1844. I like to imagine it – sails flapping against the wind, the clank of metal and groan of timber and over it all the whoosh and slap of the sea, and all that rigging and canvas slipping under quietly, like a drowning child. Then men rowing away from their vessel's terrifying disappearance, thanking their God for survival, turning their gazes towards a shore where strange limestone fingers seemed to be pointing up at him.

The wreck was located not far from here in 1970. Not that I was aware of it, being too busy taking little notice of everything but myself, and Ross whom I had not long known. It was an American whaling ship, as it happens, but Spain, the country stowing away on its name, had already been mapped onto the town, so now these are the Cervantes Islands sticking out of the Indian Ocean to the south, and street names like Seville, Majorca, Madrid and Toledo record the accidental, roundabout arrival of a mistake on our shore, making the cluster of small houses and fishing cottages sound grander than it is.

Walking along the beach this time, I muse — a bit frantically — about how personal the consequences of history are, remembering how in 1970 I chose a course of study because the blurb told me that in *Don Quixote* most experts would agree Cervantes wrote the first novel, and I lived here, and was a reader, and curious, and no more sensible choice was thrusting itself upon me for a future. All these years later, everywhere I look seems trapped in one kind of misrecognition or another and I find slippage everywhere.

These days the connection seems to have more to do with an idea of Don Quixote as some wonderful exemplar of the re-imagined, re-invented self. I am suddenly glad to have read Cervantes, suspect *quixotic* is a word I might not otherwise have appreciated at this moment, feel grateful to be walking along here with a sense of being in its very grip. It all helps. Perhaps something quixotic enters the bloodstream when you grow up in such a place. On the drive in just now, windmills seemed to be waving, literarily, and in my imagination I returned the gesture — a making of meaning to keep sadness at bay. In fact, silliness of one kind or another seems like a way forward, as I prepare myself for our coming departure on yet another quest that is really Ross's.

But all other options would be untenable.

So, feet sinking into soft damp sand, I find myself considering how a place contrives to make you, you. And by means so unpredictable that even a nineteenth-century wreck can seem to have had something to do with it, as if it had refused to be ignored, had been delivering a message intended for you.

This is the Turquoise Coast, I remind myself, *to which we are here to say goodbye*. Making my way along one of its white seaweed-strewn beaches, I find shafts of winter sun have even the colour of the ocean leaping into my thoughts – in the form of my modest collection of turquoise jewellery, as it happens, turquoise being my birthstone. The collection began on a journey through Arizona, where I bought a Navajo pendant at a roadside stall. Not that I would wear this now: it would feel ostentatious, mutton dressed-up as lamb, as my mother used to put the phrase, providing a straitjacket for my mature spirit. But I have saved such things for Kate and Nan, who do not want them yet, probably never will they are so unlike me.

Ross eventually stopped hurtling past Navajo stalls in the desert that day. I can still see him gripping the steering wheel.

'Okay, Lili. Jewellery!' His expression was saying, *I hate this situation too, and I'll do anything right now to please you, appease you.*

'No, not just jewellery,' I snapped, unrelenting. 'Turquoise, so meaningful to me. Signs, keepsakes, mementos, we need them. Don't worry, I won't break the bank.'

He sighed. 'I'm not thinking of money, Lilith. It's just, they know you're a tourist. That's who all this stuff's for, you realise. I doubt any of it's authentic.'

'And they're right. I've turned into the perpetual tourist. Ask the Canadian government. I can't even get a proper visa, so no social security number, so I *can't* work. *I'm* not authentic. I've become an eternal visitor. And I'll never understand how I could have been stupid enough to put myself in this situation.'

At least we must have been speaking.

That pendant turned out to be real turquoise and for years I felt resplendent when I wore it. Now it will be stored away with other remnants, at a warehouse in Kewdale, while we begin a new life, a new chapter of this life.

I try to shake off persistent melancholy about how many places can never be revisited and now the accident of those that will, at moments feeling desperately uncertain about the prospect of leaving home again. I squint into the light – that sand, this sand, the colour of the sea – try to concentrate on the fact that under this glorious ocean, away from which I must tear myself, all manner of industrious beauty is going about its unselfconscious business. Among the perforations and indentations of the coast, nudibranchs are moving across reef floors like small bright surprises. I try to imagine them: vivid turquoise sea slugs with orange and black bands tracing the pattern of their undulations as they make their way. They have gorgeous cousins going about their submarine business over at Rottnest Island, which I can just make out on the horizon and where I would give anything to be spending a day before we leave.

Except, time. Time is running. Running out.

I have needed this: Hansen Bay, Ronsard Bay; the clarifying wind, the smell and feel of it are a comfort. Hardly the first soul-searching Ross and I have done here, of course. This beach has heard me shout and seen me cry; the wind has blustered my thoughts into shape along this stretch of sand for as long as I can remember. Tilting into it, I look back to where Ross is photographing. The sky over Thirsty Point is turning violet, a storm moving in.

He calls out and his voice floats away, but I see what he is pointing at, a scene choreographed by the wind, cray boats pulling on their anchors all facing out to sea at exactly the same angle as the gulls on the beach are standing.

Ross waits, takes my hand, his thumb absently tracing my wayward lifeline to where it ends in the knot of damaged flesh at my wrist – that mark of an old misery – and again and again, a habit it took me years to stop minding so much I would pull away from him. We walk to the end of one of the jetties for a closer look at a couple of dolphins making lazy arcs around the boats. Storm signs are of no consequence to them; their wet backs surface in curves and gleam like the rubber tyres slapping the sides of the jetty as waves slop through.

Leaning on an anchor to watch them, and feeling its rough skin, I realise how much I have learned to like rust, the chains around a pylon, a metal plate on old timbers, the henna-coloured surface of poles, all submitting to corrosive sea air. *Should I ever come back to live here*, I think – recklessly, because I never will, not enough years left to do it in, no matter how unrealistic I let myself be about a human life span – *I would not fight the wind*. The paint on my house would be allowed to peel, timbers would be allowed to weather, there would be no fierce struggle against salt, to grow roses so you appear respectable, or crops to prolong a family burden. I would live as close as possible to the sea and walk these beaches every day in all weather. I would collect whatever bits and pieces wash in as if the ocean had been eating and were spitting out the bones. I might even cover my house with shells, stones, glass and driftwood, give in to sea and wind inside a carapace of my own making. Cervantes is a town where you could survive such eccentricity.

I doubt I will ever be brave enough to unleash the self who has whispered like this at me all my adult life. In that scenario there is no Ross – the untenable thought, but then thoughts are often reckless of their own accord.

Mine turn to my brother, Martin, and his wife, Cherry, tucked up in Mandurah in their fine house, their lives groomed, watered and well-nourished behind high limestone walls. Of the generations of men who tried to make a go of it here, Martin was the one who lived through the giving up, and losing the farm was hard on him. But Cherry, sensible woman that she is, has turned adversity into triumph, loss into escape, and now Martin is an easy going man out from under the grim self-denial of all those farmers in whose shadows he grew up. Anyway, there would have been no one for him to leave a farm to when his turn came. He has no children. One way or another he was meant to be the last. I am relieved to be leaving a Cervantes from which my brother is absent, living in comfort elsewhere, not struggling, persevering, following in that tradition of wasting away.

Ross intercepts my smile to myself. 'What?'

'Oh, the other night, when I told Martin and Cherry we're off again. Did you see the look on their faces? It was even funnier when I wouldn't rule out ever coming back up here to live.'

'They might be right. It'd be tough in this wind.'

'Of course we won't. I just didn't want to say never.'

'Heartland,' Ross says. 'We've often come here to make the big decisions.'

We both know this could be the last Cervantes sees of us.

Around the point a couple of oystercatchers keep us company, following like dogs until we all stop at the bleak carcass of a decapitated turtle. I run my hand over the devastated creature's perfect shell. It seems like a coincidence to be finding it washed up here when I have just thought of that odd word, *carapace* – I like to notice this kind of trivial prescience, as if the action of synchronicity in life might actually be felt and whatever flow it is I persuade myself I'm going with might be detected. A shred of orange nylon rope is caught in unkempt turtle tissue at the neck and the great shell under my hand seems terribly squandered, as well as grisly.

'Hard to imagine how it could have happened.' Ross says, as willing as I am to think about something other than leaving.

We start making our way back to the car. The birds stay.

We are here to say goodbye to the past itself, that's the thing. There are no people to farewell any more, but I am keenly aware of the old house out there, empty, leaning before the wind. Ross is right: territory of child-hood, stamping ground, backdrop to the beginnings of our marriage, perfect place in which to be having this conversation that could determine the rest of our lives. Not that we are actually having it yet, but should, must, will, and I am waiting for Ross to begin.

When the sun comes out again what country we live in is suddenly irrelevant and oceans seem like a blue-green planetary trick. Beneath them the earth's uninterrupted terrestrial surface seems generous and whole, and I tell myself all places are connected and there is only a splendid, rippling continuity.

Beginnings are in here somewhere, Cervantes being Lilith's place of origins. She has also reached the point of knowing selves are many, and notices she minds less and less that some of hers are receding, even though on days like today they reel away in her memory like pennants in a high wind.

I am tempted to proceed by describing my floating fishwife self in the third person in this way, to perform that act of imagining that I have stepped out and turned her into someone else, that old game, which in my case could begin with something like this: 'Lilith finds it impossible to think of herself in the third person, so she does not, thinks of herself as I, while concocting this story about a woman who is both her and not her at all. We have come to expect this dissimulation.'

Not that she means to avoid telling the truth, but some telling is out of the question and not all truths are worth telling in the first place. If it were possible to enter anyone's head at a random moment, you would find yourself privy to the banal, mundane, absolutely ordinary. Lilith is no exception and there are wells in her story like everyone else's, and like most people she goes on falling into them, even now that regarding herself as orphaned ought to be out of the question.

It is possible therefore – could thought be intercepted – that at any given moment Lilith might be thinking along such lines as these: how she has read that when addiction rattles in families the children take on certain roles and in adulthood may regard themselves as special. So thinking, possibly, about how she acted a part on behalf of her family, always striving; how she tried for too long to be valiant at things for which she had no aptitude, like singing in an eisteddfod that time, or playing the piano in a fairground competition, or grimly competing in the loathed sporting carnivals – once winning fairest and best at netball, an event so startling it is branded on her memory. Or how at different times – and at one point all at the same time – she was girl guide, marching girl, child of Mary, police club gymnast and alto in the choir. And how, in the hope of cleaning up her father's act and determined to save his soul, she went to Mass every morning for years and in grade six squeezed as many novenas into twelve months as it was possible to make on Father Ryan's rocky schedule, which developed in her a habit of counting and made nine her favourite number.

Until she rejected all that and grew up. It happened in that order.

At school Lilith was not a high achiever, except in her one-trick subject. For this she achieved childhood honours that called her to the stage on speech nights, a small accolade that made her dedicated to proving the worth of the people who had conceived her, because each time they were fit to burst with pride, unaware that winning an award for art rated like winning an award for religious studies, or home economics. It was nothing like winning prizes for maths, science, or even English, which at least suggested you could read, and probably spell, at a time when spelling correctly was a virtue. Nevertheless, because of these moments of distinction she became determined to console her parents by becoming a something, although she was never sure what that ought to be. Still isn't.

The trivial successes became levers for pushing aside other facts, like that there were nights when her father did not come home and in a black rage her mother could transform into a shrew. In that household love had an edge to it. It could be taken for granted, but something was being compensated for, always.

Or, entered into randomly like this, Lilith's thought trajectories could be more to do with forms of compensation, like why art became the particular straw she clutched at. Still does.

The thing is, I could draw, so year after year at school I won the art prize and was replaced on that influential stage only once. Even now I am closer to being an old woman than the girl who was sick the night Deirdre Crocker walked across the stage in her stead – some things you never forget – I cling to the idea of my modest artistic gift. I had spent half that term in bed with mysterious stomach-aches, a symptom of longing to leave school. The nuns sent me home to get over it and, removed from school, I did.

Orbits shifted. I would sit up in bed drinking in the unfamiliar surroundings home turned out to be during term, as if I was somehow catching sight of my own absence. I spent whole days listening intently to that hush. I did jigsaw puzzles by the hour, can feel myself running my fingers over a surface when it was complete, how something in that settling of shapes, that neat, tactile pleasure, attached itself to me, how I would dive into a new box, examine all those pieces with their bubble-limbs and open mouths, all crucially different so you knew when you were forcing them together.

There is nothing like the satisfaction of right pieces fitting, a satisfaction I get now from a fine mosaic surface, the thing that brings real contentment. Those puzzles were a beginning, with their thatched-roof cottages set in the Cotswolds, fleets of yachts on the Mediterranean, scenes of alpine grandeur, all feeding a desire to see The Outside World, a phrase that punctured the speech of the nuns who taught me, causing my imagination to leak.

Or, Lilith could be thinking that to the outside world – and to have been a child then in isolated Cervantes was to have inhabited a peculiar ambivalence that the world was elsewhere and at the same time that Cervantes was the whole world – hers was like any other battling rural family.

At thirteen the kids were shipped off, as their mother put it, to boarding school, where nuns – for the most part earnest Irish girls whose own mothers must have been astonished at where their daughters had ended up – called them love-ly: 'such a love-ly big family, such love-ly children, your love-ly little mother'. It almost rhymed with godly the way they said it, and the falling intonation was to convey approval, because all four Healy offspring – two boys and two girls, (girl, boy, girl, boy), a fine Catholic symmetry – were passing through their schools. So the nuns could rest assured souls had been saved in this little colonial nest, which made them feel better about themselves, indeed superior for the first time in their lives. By the time they were done everyone in this family would go to Mass on Sundays, except our father, but on behalf of

God nuns forgave farmer fathers lapses in faith. They were men. They had work to do.

It was the 1950s. Among my father's generation, men losing themselves in the consolations of booze was a common form of despair. By nature he was a good-humoured and gentle man, so we loved him despite the binges into which he could disappear for days on end. My mother, god rest her soul, *was* lovely – no other word for it – did her best when he unleashed his guilty conscience on her afterwards.

Once, deciding it was a good time for a fresh start, she threw a party for my father's birthday and took the drastic step of inviting neighbours.

'Surpri-ise!' She was sparkling with rare self-congratulation.

But he only looked around the room and, flushing with shyness that nearly always flew out of him as rage, turned on her, saying, 'Don't ever do anything like this again.'

He walked out, leaving her scarlet, wounded, passing around cake and pretending, hopelessly, that she found it funny, in an effort to put everyone else at ease. She would do her crying later, on the verandah, in the dark.

From which verandah that was one of many nights I watched my father's tail-lights dwindle among the trees at the corner where the fence wire had unravelled. Gravel dust was settling in moonlight long after his car had disappeared. All I could tell her was, 'He turned left, Mum,' at which her lips drew into the tight line that meant he had headed to Perth and we would not see him for a week.

Since thought is involuntary, Lilith could easily be caught in the act of thinking about such a night, since it was one of *those* moments and comes back, uncalled for, a bubble in a memory that fizzes. She had plenty of these, got over them, has spent the usual amount of a lifetime flung between believing she had the good fortune of the unhappy childhood and knowing it was an ordinary mixture of miseries and joys. By this time, of course, she is aware that they were an altogether unremarkable family and her insecurities were nothing more than a side effect of being an oversensitive child too attuned to a loved mother's feelings, but the past comes back of its own accord, always in bits and pieces, always with Cervantes in the background.

At any moment Lilith could just as easily be thinking instead, therefore, of a popular notion you come across in magazines and on television, about glory doing a hero child no good, how she comes to believe she is inauthentic and will never be convinced she is clever, good or talented, but becomes obsessed by seeming to be so, because her role is to keep up appearances. By implication, the performance is always hollow. The more she achieves, the emptier it seems, and the closer she feels to exposure.

Thought being like an iceberg with an invisible mass supporting it, all this explains why Lilith can be found in Calgary now with the particular thought crossing her mind that it is just as well she has not covered herself with glory, then, since it would never have done a speck of good. Because cover herself with glory she has not.

And this is why she is keeping watch in a snow-filled window here, pondering how to invent yet another life out of empty time stretching ahead, time into which she has to fall. At least this time she can apply for a working visa, which ought to be promising at least. Although the stories about how few prospects there are for a woman of her age are in the very air, not to mention the obstacle of her un-Canadian qualifications, which could be almost insurmountable.

When you move with your children, you can devote yourself to being their mother. You join wifely associations, propel yourself into lunches, book clubs, card afternoons, badminton, engage in competitive dressing and social jostling on behalf of the careers of husbands, out of which friends are inevitably found. You find an art class, exercise class, learn to skate, ski, meditate. You further your education. You volunteer. She has done it all, knows you must to extract a sense of meaning from baggy time that comes of having only domestic responsibilities, knows how the week days must be improvised.

Not that improvising is in any way lamentable. It is, after all, how she comes to be here with a securely taped box nearby containing the tools of her craft, which have become for her like amulets, charms, fetishes. But this time just how to proceed – the best next step, at her age – is not yet self-evident.

So she still has these moments of feeling stripped of confidence, and the old matters pass through her mind in the way of emotional detritus with its fragments and chips of experience and slivers of self-awareness collected over a lifetime's worth of waiting in hairdressing salons and doctors' and dentists' offices, where she has learned to accept that she is anything but special.

Since in reality we cannot see into other people's heads, I abandon such attempts to convert myself into someone else. Any such Lilith would be a fiction, a word, whereas I am alive and ordinary in this place where I find myself being alive and ordinary – can't say truer than that. And one truth is that along the way Ross plucked me from a nondescript tangle of circumstances and there have been consequences.

Life is partly a matter of luck, and Ross has been my great stroke of it. Not that I would presume to try summing him up. No matter how long they live in each other's company, people remain mysteries to each other in essential ways.

Nor do I mean to have encapsulated the lives of my parents; it would be like pinning them alive to a board and reducing their existence to that agony. They were ordinary lovers, a woman and a man just as often happy as not, who would have been wounded to discover a daughter of theirs has the kind of sensibility that attaches itself to bad times. Some things are private, even from one's children, especially from one's children, so when it comes to my parents I know nothing about a lot.

In other words, there are many ways of becoming an ordinary woman, all imperfect. That is to say, I speak only for myself and as I do am missing Ross, who seems suddenly and unexpectedly to be on a rig out in the North Atlantic instead of in the outback somewhere. I miss our daughters. Sitting in this floor-to-ceiling window, I gaze out onto a city on the verge of a freezing night the like of which I have experienced, but not for many years. Snow blurs the lights of the Husky Oil building; streams of headlights stall and cross at traffic lights fifteen floors below; buildings, cars, people, steaming like so many dragons. I sit for what seems like hours in a silence you can almost touch, missing everyone I have ever known.

It is hardly surprising that a dead turtle should trigger recollections between us about an earlier time when a dwarf minke whale had beached itself, how we walked the beach for a long time that day too, only stopping when the stench of the whale's carcass was like hitting a wall. It was May, I am certain, because we had only recently arrived back from India and had just discovered I was pregnant with Kate. We were in Cervantes to break the news to my parents and walked up and down along here preparing.

Mine was to be a brave speech about our generation being free of convention. It was destined to become defiant and tearful. Ross's contained words like *honourable*, and was conciliatory and hopeful and full of futile desire to avoid putting more grief in my parents' faces. Kate took care of us all by being born. Won their hearts, soothed their furrowed brows, assuaged – as much as it could ever be – the other sorrow, the great sorrow of losing Margaret and Dougal that would never leave them and that I barely understood at the time.

The whale, a female about three metres long, lay on the beach like a warning. I was convinced life had taken a turn over which I had no control, that I too had lost my bearings.

Now I can look at Ross these nearly four decades later and wonder at how wrong I was, but am aware of walking in the footsteps of that girl fearing her own stranding, have a heightened sense of her here on the beach, ahead of me. The turtle seems just as full of portent, as if at significant times the sea really does bring messages, only I don't speak its language, so it can tell me nothing that will help.

Inevitably, Ross and I end up talking all over again about the *Kirki* as well, on our way back to the car. How before the crippled ship lost its bow near Esperance, all those thousands of miles south, it was stricken not far from here and the first of nearly eight thousand tonnes of its spilled oil hit the sea between here and Jurien Bay. When it happened we were living in Canada, so we reminisce about how Kate and Nan reacted, declaring home a disaster area. That year they both did school projects on the *Kirki*, of which no one in Canada had heard, and later the *Exxon Valdez*, about which no one had not.

For such reasons our daughters grew up diligent about the health of the planet, desiring to be always everywhere at once saving it. Ross and I only have to look at each other to understand some of the activism that sends them packing across the world, but we have compromised, ended up, our lives never quite matching the ideals and convictions with which we started out. Among the things we have got right though, Kate and Nan are the best.

The thought prompts me to wonder where they are right now, precisely what they might each be doing, seeing, feeling, a habit of mind since it seems we are destined to live so far apart. I manage the grief seeping through the divisions in my world, but I can never staunch it entirely. As their father and I walk back up the beach we have walked on countless occasions, this time contemplating a sudden turn in our own futures and trying to come at the daunting conversation pragmatically, the wish flits through me that my daughters have found themselves wonderful lovers.

Ross keeps declaring it a godsend that I am not working, trying to console me for the litany of frustrations my working life has been, and here comes the next. I want to argue, old hat, that what I do every day *is* work, but I know what he means.

'Yes, but your journeys are always a form of progress and mine trail losses,' I say.

It has all been said before. The conversation generally grows into mutual reassurances that the future is curled up in the present and may well be something to look forward to, always on the trail of a silver lining. We have read our share of guides to positive thinking. Ross knows I will make the usual accommodations.

From the beach we drive out to the Pinnacles. My father used to love this road. An institution is fresh in my mind, where he is physically strong but forgetting everything, not far from Cherry and Martin so they can keep an eye on him. He hadn't the faintest idea who Ross and I were when we visited this time, was irritable, snapping at the nurse that he was in no mood for meeting people, quick to be aggressive and rude in a way he rarely used to be. Resemblances blur his memories. This time he decided Martin was his brother, Tom, who never came home from the Second World War. He kept inviting him to play cricket out the back.

'Just need the weather to clear up, Tom,' he said repeatedly, at which Martin hunched further into his cardigan. The day never did become fine enough for our father to lift his rangy frame from that chair into which he seems to have sunk forever.

I find myself wondering how you can lose so much and remain so apparently intact. Big chunks of absence have been responsible for taking other memories away altogether. I, more out of sight and mind, keep being erased, so he keeps meeting me for the first time. The rest of the family, Margaret and Dougal, even our mother, would be nowhere to be found, just filed away somewhere deep inside him as sadness.

It is not a good time to be leaving; I may never see my father again. This is the kind of thought I can only defend myself against by dismissing, however, although I ought to know better. Absence takes various forms, I tell myself, trying to be consoled by the knowledge that he won't miss me, he can't.

The drive takes us through town, where we pass a line of tiny Japanese women pouring from a bus. They fight flapping coats and scarves and stare up at the tanks on the water tower, trying to appear interested in what a guide is telling them about water towers. People come from all over the world these days, so the town has responded with a backpackers' hotel and the functional motel where Ross and I will spend tonight, not to mention the tour buses that make their survival possible by rolling through almost daily.

It seems strange to be hearing foreign languages in our few straggly streets, but beyond them is oh-my-god country, wide and compelling, and alien no doubt, unless you grew up in it, so people come to gaze. They shade their eyes like these diminutive women, walk around for a while, try to imagine living here, perhaps, and I daresay cannot. Whereas I am finding it impossible to absorb the fact that this is the last time I may see the water tower for years – at my age, possibly ever. I have a sudden sense of lives intersecting here and veering away, and everything ordinary seems extraordinary, as if I have new eyes. It is always like this when we about to leave.

Being late winter, the native wisteria is blooming. Its midnight blue sprinkles the road to the Pinnacles. Soon the scrub will flash with red, purple, orange, yellow and white. The drive through Nambung is a drive through more than a thousand species. In spring it becomes another place. Not that our wildflowers are flamboyant: to see most of them you have to walk, stoop, look down, take time, be willing to wander, otherwise subtle beauties escape and only the rush of blue-greens into summer is visible, when the place is immersed every year in hot, dry-grass variations on gold.

At the Pinnacles Ross and I mean to follow a path we have often walked, but the tourist bus has followed us out, so instead we head for the edge, to where you can look north up the Batavia Coast stretching towards Kalbarri. Batavia, Cervantes: I feel the history of the world bumping against the shore, savour the fact more the older I get.

We walk aimlessly. The thicker pinnacles are like manicured tips of submerged mountains making a forest of stone spikes stretching away through the dunes, as far as you can see once you are among them. Some are just fingers, centimetres high, with yellow sands sifting around them like false promises. It is a grave landscape, the earth subsiding around its own bones, a slowly disclosing skeleton of monumental proportions evoking a sense of monumental time.

'See the contest?' Ross interrupts my reverie. 'Lime-stone formation versus the windblown quartz sands of the Spearwood dunes. That's why the sand's so yellow. It blows off to reveal the Pinnacles, just a dune system travelling across ancient vegetation.'

He has said all this before but never tires of it. Such elucidations are a feature of his generosity. Hands plunged into his pockets and hunched against the cold wind, my lovely husband *now*, silver in his hair, making new plans to keep us all safe. The sun comes out between clouds and throws his long shadow across damp turmeric-coloured earth.

'I used to pretend they were the shadows of archangels when I was a child,' I tell him. 'I still think the place drones with something mystical.'

History is about to repeat itself and we have to decide which it should be. We spend a good hour walking before Ross gets to the point, predicts the project he has been working on will go ahead eventually but an American company will run the show.

'The government never really trusts the local expertise,' he says, a new bitter edge to his voice, 'despite submission after submission to demonstrate it and all their protestations to the contrary. I just can't stand the thought of being on a pension when I'm old. Not that there'll *be* pensions for the likes of us anyway,' he adds. 'At least not until we've lost pretty much everything we've worked for first.'

We.

The story is not all bad. Despite looming financial insecurity I can feel Ross's relief that the job has petered out. He has been hanging on, has spent too long battling on behalf of a company in which belligerence and one-upmanship are being called a skill set. Loyalty is out of style. Definitions of success are in flux. Ruthlessness is disavowed but seems to dominate corporate shenanigans more and more, so I decide it must just be invisible to those who perpetrate it. All around us ethics seem to be increasingly mistaken for sentiment, and the glib notion that there should be no sentiment in business drives negligent, overindulged men and women who over third and fourth glasses of scotch can easily convince themselves that decisions they made that day are excellent only because they made them. More and more have too little regard for the effects of what they decide on other people, the world – that way weakness.

Perhaps I am a cynic and Ross and I are out of touch. In any case, this is something of the context out of which our fork in the road emerges: Dubai or Calgary, Calgary or Dubai – although the overworked enigma collapses, since both are roads we have already taken, a fact of our history that seems only to hamper the decision.

'Amazing to think of things we've seen and done since the first time you and I walked along here together,' Ross says, taking my hand and bringing an end to these ruminations.

'And now we have to choose between ferocious heat and intense cold, deserts versus glaciers. Why do the two options have to be so extreme?' I say, for a moment wanting to resist his cheerfulness, his jockeying along.

'We have to keep making a living. Anyway, I know which I'd prefer,' he adds, maintaining a positive spin on things. 'Skiing again. The mountains, Banff…' Then he turns to me. 'We're not people of independent means, I'm afraid, Lili, but who is?'

He *is* afraid. I am the only person who knows how deep Ross's concern is that necessity should be driving our situation at this stage of our lives.

We had reason to expect otherwise, but so did plenty of people. We are children of the 1970s who have a vestigial capacity for counting blessings and generally try to muster some kind of submission to the universe, with varying success.

I try a joke. 'So, Calgary, Dubai or penury.'

He only begins thinking aloud. 'Kate and Nan can visit easily in either case, so that'll be okay, but Calgary might be better for lots of reasons. Let's face it, going back has more than nostalgia value, and the job pays more, so we wouldn't stay away as long.' He turns to me. 'I worry about you though.'

'Same as for you.'

'It seems like a last chance for me, and I don't mean that to be emotional blackmail.'

'Last year from all my bits and pieces I earned the grand, rounded-up sum of...what? Not enough to pay our private medical cover. And if we've got too little to retire on, as you say...'

'Whatever that means.'

'You're right, it's time to be realistic. We have grey hair, but we can do this.'

'So we take the job overseas, make another adventure of it, then come home and settle down here.'

'Not here.'

One minute I am counting my blessings, the next I feel compelled to leave. There is too much freedom, and none.

'Details to be decided when the time comes,' Ross says. 'Let's just follow our noses for a while.'

On the surface it has a flat rhythm, this question of roads, is finally a choice of this or that, here or there, and in the end a straightforward buying of tickets. Arriving at a decision was simple and complicated, therefore, a pleasant paradox and another example of how complicit I always am in creating my own confusions.

At some point I say to Ross, 'Tossing a coin makes sense at times like this, or consulting a psychic, or throwing a Ching. When you don't have any idea what really would be best.'

'I'm more into plus–minus analysis myself,' Ross says. 'But you're right, there's probably no good or bad decision. Once it's made go with it, give it everything we've got. Okay?'

I want to convince him. 'A line in the sand seems invigorating. Wherever it is, it'll be a fresh start. I think there's gypsy in my blood.'

The words work like an incantation, launch me into memories of living near the Rocky Mountains. The moment has arrived when I can start talking myself into the inevitable, begin making plans, for contentment among other things. If we return to Calgary and the girls visit us there, the move will be a reprise for them. Here my feet are, tingling with the power of childhood places. Call and response and call, I think, and how wonderful if Kate and Nan could dance this tango too.

I am far too inhibited to dance a tango in fact, but caught in the memory like this, life can seem like a suspension of the self into postures, slices of a rhythm, each a cross-section of some long pattern, every step adding to a series of jagged moments that make up a lovely sequence of memories – something better than stolid slow motion any way, a series of composures. For a second at the Pinnacles that day I could imagine capturing some of mine in frame after frame, had a vivid sense of a high-heeled former self, arms above her head, stamping out a rhythm, sexy and unpredictable. She almost seemed to be waiting in the shadows to begin again.

And she must be somewhat wise having known grief and joy, I assure myself, looking back. Perhaps she will have something fresh and fabulous to show her daughters, if their lives can be orchestrated by where *we* are for a while and they do come back here to Calgary to revisit places where they were children.

Dubai we have only ever visited, whereas indelible parts of our lives already belong to this place. In either case we were facing the pleasure of learning again things once known and then forgotten. We knew coming back here would be particular. So I try to let go of lingering trepidation, try to be glad I am back where there are four seasons, where I can sit watching snow fall. Life is looping back over itself, that's all.

That day Ross snapped this photograph of me. An image of a woman in a black coat looking out to sea, her shadow and the shadows of the Pinnacles lie in the same direction, striping the sand. I took this one of him standing behind a limestone shaft. With his arms outstretched on either side, it looks as if the pinnacle has arms, and the shadow it throws belongs to an angel holding an umbrella.

We were at the rise. With those mysterious stones behind me and the ocean before me, I was penetrated by the sense of how profoundly my life belongs to that littoral, liminal country. *Home*, I was thinking again, the word rolling through me, making me ambivalent. There is no way of knowing whether the destinies of woman and angel will take them back there. In these photographs they are fragile with doubt and trying to shore each other up. It is how the marriage works.

Thinking back now, I am reminded of something I read earlier this afternoon, by Anne Carson: 'a tango (like a marriage) is something you have to dance to the end' – putting me in mind of tangos, and marriages.

From the Pinnacles we drive back along Grey Road on our way out to Lake Thetis. Ross picked me up on this very road and has a story that my legs were responsible, that from where he used to sit in the university library near the stairs, in among the leg-fall passing, as he has put it far too many times, a particular pair of legs would appear. After a while he looked forward to them, and then found himself waiting for them. He likes to say he couldn't believe his luck when they turned up out here in the bush, walking along Grey Road in denim shorts, just as he happened to be driving out from Cervantes of all places. I catch a disconcerting glimpse of myself as a body on a pair of legs like stilts whenever he tells the tale. I become a crane or a heron.

I recognised him from campus, had noticed him too, but never felt noticed, not until then.

'What on earth are you doing out here?' he asked.

'I live here.'

'You're kidding!' He looked around, theatrically, in a way that has become utterly familiar.

'That's my car back in the ditch. You must have passed it.'

He misinterpreted my blush. 'Hey, look, you'll need a lift. It's way too hot to walk.' It was the first time he would ever open a car door for me.

Not that I have ever asked Ross to describe those legs. Reality can never measure up to tales a man tells to entertain his daughters, and it is impossible to communicate to each other what it is of bodies that can initiate a lifetime together.

Ross's legs are slim and beautifully shaped, a long cedilla, and as familiar to me as any legs I can think of, since both Kate and Nan have inherited them and when they all stand side by side bare-legged, their shared shape is a mystery made flesh. It is Ross's long legs that make him tall, and the hair on his legs and arms has a red sheen in sunlight that bespeaks his Viking ancestry, of which his family is proud and whence comes Kate's red hair.

I see him in my mind's eye now, legs apart, naked, drying himself after a shower, vigorously rubbing at hair that curls damply against his thighs, completely unselfconscious, my gaze having become like a blind mirror. I try to imagine his legs next to mine in bed, or when he lies on top of me, or I on top of him, how I feel the brush of his legs against mine reminding me of the difference between us, and of all that comes next. Our legs have been entwined naturally and deliberately for almost a lifetime now, in which time he has become all this to me: love, sex, pleasure, comfort; maleness, masculinity, man;

that which is other, the irreducible difference of which so much has been made – whatever it is and wherever it exists, somewhere beyond sexual politics, sometimes glimpsed in a lover's eyes.

I have looked at Ross countless times and been struck by the depths of our separateness. *I am not you* is a thought that still has the power to enchant, easily becomes a desire to say, *Come here, you.* He has been the great force for tenderness, generosity, consideration and kindness in my life. His body has loved and lifted and caressed and held and washed and consoled mine. Mine has borne his children – indelible labour of love, no matter what doctors may tell us about having no memory for pain. The result, as it turns out, is this mutual symbiosis that never ceases to astonish me and yet is so perfectly ordinary. We have become These Two, You Two, Those Two. Ross'n'Lilith. Lilith'n'Ross. You and I. Us. We.

I miss him. We should be here unpacking all this together.

Driving back along Grey Road from the Pinnacles to Lake Thetis, my thoughts afloat, it becomes possible to believe it won't matter where we go, as long as we go there together.

Lake Thetis is where we had the first real conversation of our lives, about stromatolites as it happens, which may seem unromantic, but that would be a superficial judgement, since stromatolites are among the earliest forms of life on earth and still grow there. Slowly, slowly: a third of a millimetre a year. These ones are two thousand years old or so, which Ross insists is young in fact, since the earliest stromatolites formed three and a half billion years ago. They have almost disappeared from oceans, but it seems particular blue-green algae in our little lake nurture them as they harden layer upon layer in its intense salinity. Oxygen is added to the atmosphere as they go on like ancient forests paying their way, helping us have the wherewithal to breathe. As Ross says every time we are there, a marvel of nature.

Heading out this particular day he explains for the umpteenth time that we have the best record of them in the world. 'They're alive, you know. God, it's like greeting the world as it was when life began.'

'Living fossils, you might say.'

'Yeah.'

'You have. Said it I mean.'

He grins.

We arrive at the lake to find there has been so much rain the stromatolites are submerged. Ross's disappointment, even though he must have half-expected it, brings me close to tears, although there is more to my fragility than depth of water.

He summons his usual stoicism. 'Well, it's not as if we don't know what they look like. One day I'll even finish those photos. Remember that little project? In the meantime, let's keep on dreaming, shall we?'

In my mind's eye are the ash-coloured mud flowers usually visible around the lake's edge, of which he began a series of black-and-white studies years earlier.

'Not a bad place to have begun falling in love,' I tell him.

He smiles and I add, 'Do I say that every time?'

'Pretty much, sweetheart, but I'd be disappointed if you didn't.'

Georgia O'Keeffe springs to mind. Not out of nowhere: it is only days since I watched the film of an interview in which she spoke of living in cities for thirty years despite feeling that she was never an urban woman. When Joseph Stieglitz died she moved to New Mexico, into a particular house with a door she said she had for years wanted to live behind.

'I just had to own that door,' she told the interviewer.

A Stieglitz-attack followed about her having been prevented from going there sooner, but she looked directly into the camera without a trace of defensiveness, saying crisply, 'Nonsense, there was never a question of sacrifice. It was never sacrifice. I was always simply where I had to be.' Words to that effect.

As we head back to town, putting the lake behind us, I feel the ferocious gaze of Georgia O'Keeffe directed at me, as if to convey that were I really interested in questions of wasted time I would immediately stop thinking of time spent as time wasted.

It makes sense that Georgia O'Keeffe's remark should have come back to me at Lake Thetis. Her admonition was diverting me from self-pity. Recollections of the last time we had lived in Calgary were streaming through my assurances to Ross. *No excuses this time*, I was instructing myself, chastising the time-wasting, excuse-ridden woman she was then, weighed down by a lack of any sense of direction through the tangle of desires, possibilities and frustrations of which a life is inevitably concocted. *No subsiding into misery, no defining departure as sacrifice*, I was promising myself, knowing Ross would sustain me but wanting him not to have to, wanting more genuine side-by-sideness to the experience than we achieved last time. *Just get on with it*, I was telling myself, trying to guide necessity.

While we drove I decided that were we to come back here it would be a shared decision. I would simply be where I need to be. Now I look back on that self of a few weeks ago, resting a hand on Ross's thigh, gesture of connection of more than thirty years, and murmuring 'Love you', words that are usually code for some impulse hidden in a moment. He would have had no idea mine were full of the first time we had lived here in Canada, or that I was responding to the celluloid guidance of Georgia O'Keeffe.

It *will* be different. I insist on it. Watching snow spin through a sky made orange by city lights – snow, that ineffable embodiment of silence, it occurs to me, making the world lovely in ways I had quite forgotten – I remind myself that I always surrender eventually, it is only a matter of time.

Of which I have wasted more than I like to think about, but there I go again, losing my way. In this instance in reflections about how the very word, Cervantes, has childhood memories sifting through me, as if I am the place, how as a child there I lost hours collecting the stocks of stones and shells I used to arrange and rearrange in a rock garden I was constructing under the front steps. I remember asking my father once why I could never grow maidenhair fern successfully, and after he explained about salt in the air I dreamed of winged salt, believing it must look like snow. I can see now how little I knew about so much.

It was the early 1960s. Lift off. Boarding school, where several years' worth of Monday mornings would be spent rearranging desks in order of merit after the nuns had marked Friday tests over the weekend. Desperate girls with accomplishments not included in the awful stock take were occasionally judged to have cheated and would be humiliated. I resorted to storms of anxiety that still plague me, so I only seem able to believe I am working when I feel almost overwhelmed, have always invented some version or other of those tests for myself and after a lifetime still associate work more with grim effort than pleasure.

At biology, history, geography, maths – subjects teachers set store by – no matter how hard she tried, that girl, Lilith, was an also-ran, her brain never delivering up all it knew. So she settled into a fair-to-middling position, where on Monday mornings she swapped desks a couple of places up and down, with Renata, Evelyn, Meredith, Gabrielle. The names come back from a weekly shuffle according to their test results, how she thought of them all collectively as the green team, a composition of yellow and blue, adrift in the overlap halfway along a spectrum dividing the illustrious from the doomed.

I can still see Renata of the full figure and crinkly black hair, a woman among girls by fourteen, withdrawn from school at sixteen to be married off to a man fifteen years her senior who had applied to her father for the role of husband and been accepted. How awed the rest of us were by that marital prospect. Evelyn played the violin and was practising her musical way through years of being overlooked in classrooms. Meredith's daydreaming would become obsessiveness that turned her into a lean choreographer, more widely known in the end for the anorexia that almost killed her than the talent that had brought her public attention in the first place. Gabrielle, so nervous she was allergic to her own hair, would grow up to devote herself to the causes of stricken animals. So I have heard at least, grapevines and school reunions being what they are. No one tested for these talents.

Lilith's particular aptitude was on the syllabus, so her light was picked up through chinks in the bushel under which she was keeping it tucked. But the messages were mixed. The holy tyrants binding her to an idea of capital 'A' Art were also pounding it into her head that she was born for obscurity.

Hard to be a hero child when you are a one-trick pony, so she learned to gallop and gallop and gallop to please.

'A lady makes sure she has time to get from point A to point B, Miss.' It is a question mark in black serge, with its hands on its hips.

'Healy. Lilith.'

'And where are you from Miss Healy, Lilith, that you would treat this playground as a place for your vulgar running in?'

'Cervantes.'

'Sir where?'

'Sir-van-tees,' I enunciated carefully. 'Well, near there, north-east of the town.'

Her response took me by surprise. 'Bold girl! Just who do you think you are?'

'Lilith. Lilith Healy,' I repeated stupidly.

Aside to herself, as if I were deaf – or not – exasperation revealing her habitual dislike of us, me: 'The devil's concubine or some such pagan thing. It explains a great deal of course…'

Naturally, I was blushing. When words did come at such times, they would burst from me of their own accord. But I tried to defend my good name.

'She was Adam's first wife in the Hebrew tradition, my mother says. And an Assyrian goddess. And another goddess's owl. Mum says it's *mellifluous*, she loved the sound of it.'

'The sound of it, *Sister*! You will learn to address me correctly, my girl, and to curb that unruly tongue. Do I make myself clear? We will not stand for defiance here.'

'Yes. *Sister*.'

'You will write five hundred lines – *Adam was married to Eve*. And just to be going on with, I assure you!'

'Yes, Sister.'

I see myself trailing the plump white hands of that bride of Christ pulling and pulling at rosary beads slung from her waist until they became caught in the folds of her heavy black habit to irritate her even more. We walked towards the boarding house past plane trees in red flower, I listening to her these-peoples and who-do-you-think-you-ares until my stomach tightened into cramps that would double me over well into adulthood. I collapsed in her wake, right there in the playground. It was a solution.

Afterwards, waiting to be banned from everything she could think of – tennis, choir, the drama club, the world, heaven – I spent several hours certain of bleeding to death as a punishment for my sins. The pain did turn out to be more than the dysmenorrhoea that would plague my teenage years from then on. I was also suffering from a spastic colon, so Dr Atkinson told my mother at least, condoning my temporary escape.

It would be years before I recognised that pain for the arrival of fury. Sister was wrong. The quality I have always lacked is defiance. I am anything but bold.

School was curbing my tongue indeed, teaching me that the likes of us are all honky nuts, eucalyptus leaves, magpies, brown bread, wire fences, water tanks, dandelions and buffalo grass. There are neither convicts nor aristocrats to be excited about here. I was taught to think of myself in terms of only-ness: only a bit of Scot, a bit of Irish, a bit of Slav back there, back then, until great, great someone anglicised his name to survive in an ethnocentric Australia. My grandmother, who kept an elaborate altar to Our Lady of Perpetual Succour at her front door, used to say she could see the Slav in my nose.

'More's the pity!' she would add, teaching me to suspect my nose.

All this is partly what it is to be the daughter of a decent man who was a little ambitious for a while, then disapproved of, overlooked, disappointed, a man of good heart, whose life was weighed down by loss, but who showed me what it is to be resilient – until his mind went, but there you are. And of an insistently gentle mother I heard described once – unforgivably, by someone calling herself my friend – as *petit bourgeois*, it striking me immediately that friends should not be people who try to put you off your mother, so I learned to be more discerning, especially about friends with petty pretensions.

It was the early 1960s. It was Fremantle. Cassata had only just been heard of, we bought apple strudel at Culley's and thought ourselves sophisticated for getting a word like *strudel* off our tongues, we bought padded pointy bras at Pellews. What could any of us have been but petty and bourgeois?

Later, as a young woman, after I had begun making art on my own behalf – tentatively, painfully, but with a secret hunger for perfection that can still be my undoing – I began laying claim to life. My first course, taken incongruously but earnestly at an institute of technology, was in textiles.

For a final submission I covered a vast old armchair that looked like some great barnacled contraption retrieved from Atlantis by the time I was finished. It was my study in blue, for which I had collected material from everywhere, so even the deep ultramarine crepe of my mother's going-away dress was cut up and appliquéd onto it – in fact, was the starting point from which I moved across blue from turquoise through to indigo and violet.

It brought me a first-in-class-competition, that chair – validation, a moment of prestige, more deadly encourage-ment – and I hung onto it for years although it was too large for any corner I could find. Finally I was forced to abandon it when we moved to Canada last time, a loss for which I would be compensated by snow, icicles, mountains, deer, peonies…

I have nothing to bring to Ross's love story but this kind of ordinary profusion, and since I suppose I am his love story as much as he is mine, and if that is what being back here amounts to, then I can't help but be intrigued by an inventory that might try to sum up a *me*.

It occurs to me that it would be easier to identify myself by many things I am not. I am not exotic, for example, and however I might desire to carry off a sultry look and would give much to produce some serious fortune-telling, there is no trace of actual gypsy in these veins. I am not compelling in any way, in fact, being pink-skinned and speckled from too much time in the sun and genes that punish you for that. I flush when I drink, a disability I inherited from my mother, who called it a safety mechanism and, given my father's history, was probably right. I am neither tall nor slender nor any elegant thing, although kind people have told me I have panache, which I suspect is a flair for camouflage, also indicated by a regular impulse to change the colour and style of my hair, until recently at least.

So, in the blood I brought to the conceptions of our children there is nothing particular, or interesting, or special, or intricate, or likely to produce great beauty or talent. I am only I. Ross is only Ross. We are just this *us*, and our daughters, Katherine and Nancy Olson, two divine young women who seem like spectacular miracles to us, are, as they like to joke, therefore mongrels.

Ross and I did not meet near a gangplank at a harbour that bustles in blues and greys like a scene in a film about love and loss. We did not meet on holiday in a low-lit cocktail bar made sexy with the sound of jazz. We did not meet at Niagara Falls, or on a picket line battling injustice, or on a blind date arranged by insightful friends, or at any glittering party. We met by accident in blazing heat on Grey Road near the Pinnacles turn-off, where my car had broken down and he offered me a lift because he had seen me around at the university where we were both studying. It was not yet a dangerous time. Accepting that ride was still sensible behaviour.

Nevertheless, one thing leads to another, as my mother had foretold. On the way into town that first time Ross needed to stop at Lake Thetis, stromatolites being the subject of his dissertation and the reason he was in Cervantes. Once we got talking we discovered we had so much to say that it made sense to stop in at the pub afterwards for a cold drink, where he tried to convince me I should stop seeing our coastal country as a place from which to escape. At the end of the day he dropped me at the turn-off.

'So. Home,' he said that day too.

'Yes,' I replied, and he studied the empty paddocks and this time laughed.

'The house is over the hill,' I said, blushing again and adding, 'It's not a good time to ask you in, sorry. Anyway, I like the walk, we always do it.'

I did not say my father had not come home the night before and might reappear at any moment in his vilest manifestation. It would not have been a good beginning, and intuition was telling me something had begun. For safety's sake, I would insist on calling it friendship at first.

Now I like to think that if Ross had kissed me it would already have been a kiss to stake a claim, but he only watched me climb through the fence – near where my sister and brother were shortly to end their lives as it happens, but how impossible it is to foresee such things – and drove away with a casual wave. He tells the girls he made me wait, and that it worked.

The relationship was to take its new shape a whole year later, in Fremantle among a crowd of university students feasting on chicken and spaghetti at the Roma. Neither of us wanted to leave. Ross leaned over and kissed me a tartufo kiss, which we have delighted in ever since: balls of chocolate ice-cream rolled in crushed dry chocolate with a cream-coated cherry at the heart – not a bad metaphor for the fall into love. The really big moments were to arrive in India, about which we knew nothing then, but with that tartufo came the first inklings.

When I did get home that feast-night, it was to receive a phone call that would change everything. Margaret had been driving Dougal home for the holidays. She had missed the turn-off and the car rolled on the gravel.

They lay side by side in a chapel, a brightly lit teak-lined room as sensible as a sauna. Dougal's hair had been tamed with Californian Poppy and brushed unnaturally across a scratch on his forehead as if to hide it, but our mother smoothed it back gently, resting the back of her hand against his temple, as though checking his temperature. She couldn't bear to take her hand away. She was warming him.

He seemed smaller. They both did.

I sat twisting my grandmother's rosary beads around my fingers and pulled at them so hard they broke, along with my heart I felt, but my father helped me tuck them under Margaret's fingers anyway and arranged them so they seemed intact.

'It doesn't matter, Lilith,' he whispered several times, trying to relieve my distress, even placing an awkward arm around my shoulder, but I still think of them there, imperfect, an untidiness I hid from my orderly elder sister.

My mother insisted you should always touch your dead, so eventually I caressed Dougal's wounded temple, trying to touch him fearlessly the way she did, but only tentative and self-conscious. Martin refused. He hung back, angry and unsettled, and for a long time afterwards Martin and I would behave in each other's company as though we were embarrassed to be alive. My father watched us all in silence.

How long it is since I have felt the cool back of my mother's hand against my own as she tested my skin for health, her gesture of comfort, as though she could fuse with you to discover whether you were eating well, sleeping enough, being good.

'Don't burn the candle at both ends now, will you, dear?'

I still do it with Kate and Nan. They call it docking. A small gesture of love goes rolling through time.

That year turns into a misbehaving dream from which I wake myself crying. In it the Morris Minor is jammed against a tree at the turn-off. Dougal and Margaret are rag dolls in the back seat. My mother is draped over the steering wheel.

I have been misled by the accuracy of the nightmare: tuart trees in their proper places, their wide crowns throwing the usual lacy shade over the spot where fencing wire unravelled years earlier; the verge the same as at the turn-off, the familiar crumbling edge where bitumen gives way to gravel; the car the one that belonged to our grandmother, bearing all the marks of Martin and Dougal's hotting-up after she gave it to them, when Martin tried to teach Dougal everything he knew about engines and decided Dougal didn't have it in him; its red seats the red seats in my dream – all details perfect and plausible.

The only sign of blood is a tiny abrasion on Dougal's forehead where his head rests against the rear window. Through the dream glass I can see fine striations in the wound, am close enough to see the pores of his skin. It crosses my mind that his skin was beginning to break out and now it is broken. He is twelve.

Margaret looks as though she has fallen asleep in an awkward position. Her wrist is bent. She would have had pins and needles were she to wake up. I can see the time on her watch: four thirty-three. The second hand keeps up its flicking rotation. Her mascara has smudged in the heat.

My own voice calling through the driver's window to my dream mother wakes me up. I know straight away that I have this to face: there has been a death. But having dreamt three were dead, my mind is distorting information like the horizon in great heat. I cannot make out the thing I am looking at. Soon I am certain there have been two deaths, in fact – it seems impossible, but I am filled with a dread that could never be invented.

'Who was it who died?'

Where could anyone direct such a question, so I spend until dawn in my armchair – blue cradle of success, raft of creative promise – afloat for hours, sealed in, until it becomes clear that in reality my mother was not in the car. It also becomes clear that it was not the Morris jammed against a tree at all, it was Margaret's kombi. The facts come into focus like an appalling election on which everything depends and in which no winners were ever possible. In a great struggle with love, so that something caves away inside me that will stay gone, relief lunges at grief. The Margaret and Dougal parts of me shift. Cavities form that will be filled too easily with melancholy after this, flushing happiness away at unexpected times, leaving me watching for death and with a fragile capacity for joy.

Certain facts have provided the core of my life until this moment. I come from a family of six: mother, father, sister, two brothers. The centre must hold. Everyone will be well. Circumstances will stay the same: sure, safe where I have left them on the fringes of my day-to-day life. My family: the background music to who I am.

And so it is, still. The idea of losing Ross, Kate or Nan overwhelms me if I give it any thought, each possibility being its own terrible entity. There is no compensation or substitution or replacement to be had for any one of them, only absolute equivalence in the potential for loss. I envy people who have not had to learn this.

What had happened would be referred to in the family simply as The Accident from then on, becoming generic. I still remember it through a dream so real I can slip into believing I was there, that I stared through the window examining Dougal's forehead, noticing Margaret's wrist, when I saw no such things. When I did see them they lay side by side in the teak chapel.

I began that sorrowful morning imagining my mother through her greeting touch. By lunchtime, she had been spared to visit me in Canada years later, well after I had become a mother myself. And because of her heart, which really was broken, that is the journey that would take her.

In that future time I would come across a poem by Margaret Atwood about dreams, how they can be filled with images

not blurred or faded by dream
but exact, the way they were.
Such dreams are relentless...

It would remind me of my vivid vision of my brother's and sister's deaths all those years before, which by then had become its own kind of memory — exact but false, false but true. Reading the poem I would feel affirmed long after the event. Sitting in a house in Canada I would find myself trying to recall the faded faces of my dead brother and sister, and I would begin to understand how in time all events and impressions fuse and accuracy fails in favour of connectedness.

But on the day of their funeral, insight of every kind lay far ahead.

There is only shock and the devastating echo. That terrible duplication. A funeral exceptional for the twoness of things: two coffins side by side in a chapel where we have gathered to say the rosary, two coffins side by side at Mass next morning. Everyone looks propped up in the pews and ghastly importance hangs over being the immediate family, but there is strange consolation in the fact they died together.

'At least they were together.' The phrase is in the air; my parents take comfort from it.

Two hearses. Twelve pallbearers.

A partridge in a pear tree: it seems this absurd.

But a Requiem Mass is no time for rebelliousness. I discover how mean and irrelevant is my adolescent pop-scepticism, singing 'Make Me a Channel of Your Peace' with everyone else just because they need me to, and the hymn turns to lava in my veins.

There are slivers of precise memory. I remember the sound of bees, have an image of my white shoes on that dark soil, and of my hands as I brushed my fingers together after sprinkling it on their coffins.

Once. Twice. My mind is busy: Dougie was the baby, so he ought to go first, then Margaret will have her fistful, launched from my clean hand with its unfairly long lifeline; but Margaret was my older sister, so perhaps I should do her first and *then* Dougie, birth order – which makes me wonder about death order and how we can never know theirs. As I stand at their side-by-side graves wishing everything could be simultaneous and that everything could be done simultaneously and with my right hand, the great bleakness of that double vision envelops me.

Which is when Ross steps forward and stands beside me as if he belonged there.

'You looked like you needed someone,' he tells me when I thank him later.

My memory is also imprinted with a picture of Noel, as Margaret's coffin was being lowered. Some grief tries to hide behind a squint into the sun. It narrows its eyes now and again, like a small tic, a tiny vulnerability. It takes the shape of hands clasped too tightly behind a back. You dare not go near it. Touch it and walls will collapse and you will be blasted away.

This is how it was with Noel. Watching, I vowed to love him like a brother, determinedly, for the rest of my life. Mum, Dad and I meant never to let him slip away, because Margaret had loved him. Martin was never so sure.

I see my mother at the graveside too, my father beside her, a movement of their hands, a slight clasping and unclasping in unison. They had grown alike. They moved in rhythm, had developed the same way of standing with hands on their hips, similar ways of holding a knife and fork, reading a newspaper, climbing stairs. This synchrony showed beside their children's graves.

I hear my mother on the verandah murmuring to herself afterwards, 'Dougie, how dreadful. Just a baby really. My poor little boy.' She was cupping her face with her hands, sustaining herself, holding herself in place, a gesture of pure grief actors use in tragedies and rarely get right because it is too simple, too direct, too filled with the real to be imitated.

The circumstances were simple. Margaret had offered to pick Dougal up from school and bring him home for the holidays, said she wanted to have a chat with Mum and Dad. Noel tells us later – a form of confession – that she was intending to borrow money. He will never forgive himself for needing it in the first place and blames himself for her having made the fatal trip. Our father asks him to accept the money anyway, pleads with him not to pile loss on loss, but he refuses, and from the moment of Margaret's death sets out to achieve failure like a suicide leaping.

Eventually, the bank would claim his boat.

'He should have owned that bloody boat by now,' I overhear Martin say at some point.

The peasant genes of both sides of the family have poured into Martin. Our parents always said he was a born farmer. He only submits to the idea of fate when it is a question of aberrant weather; everything else is about vigilance, knuckling down, working until you drop. So he has never trusted Noel, thinks he speaks too often of luck.

Margaret had met Noel when he began running a boat out of Cervantes. As a fisherman, he was always as vulnerable to weather as a farmer, and his hands were every bit as rough as Martin's, but their common ground eluded my brother, who has always regarded Noel as a hippie and a loser.

'If he had what it takes, he'd be out of the grip of the banks by now,' he said. 'Then she wouldn't have needed to come up here begging. Christ, it's only one boat after all, not as if it's the frigging fleet.' I could hear Martin's own struggles with banks in his voice, but he would never admit to it.

I see Martin standing beside our parents at the funeral: stiff, shocked, his face puffy with grief.

'Dougal was my only brother,' he says to me on the way back to the terrible black cars. He is shaking by the time he opens the door to let me in. He says it again, and then again.

'What are you trying to prove, Martin? Just cry, for fuck's sake,' I reply brutally the third time, having taken up swearing quite deliberately and knowing the word coming from my mouth would be like a punch to my brother's conservative heart.

I will find anything to justify this anger. How dare we drive away and leave them buried there. Climbing into the car I notice a hole in the heel of my stocking. It seems like the last straw. Failing to make my shoe swallow the imperfection, I shred my stockings as we drive away from Karrakatta, following the disused railway line. I will concentrate on anything but what is happening.

'Just leave it alone, for god's sake,' my father snaps.

'Ross should have come with us,' I reply.

But my father pronounces some things private. 'Ross is not family,' he says. 'You hardly even know the boy.'

Martin repeats, 'Now I have no brother.'

'Now I have no sister,' I snap. 'And I don't blame Noel! And Ross is not a boy!'

Later, on the verandah at the farm, murmuring into the darkness, my mother would unwittingly trigger the dissolution.

'Poor little Dougal,' she would say again.

Noel's tone comes at her sharply. 'Margaret died too, Pat. She was young too. She's gone too.'

Our mother looks up at him, as if yanked by her hair.

Martin shouts, 'Now that's it, mate, end of the line's right there! You don't get to talk to her in that tone.'

'It's all right, Martin,' she says. 'He's upset.' She turns to Noel. 'Oh darling, Dougal was still my baby, that's all. But she was my first baby, my darling girl, of course, and your wife…' She whispers, 'Losing the children like this…I'm so very sorry life is turning out this way for us all.'

The small moment of anguish had turned inside out and ended with Martin rushing Noel and the two of them rolling around on the drive, roaring, wounded, crying, so my father had to separate them.

Anger is famously described as a stage of grief, making it seem like something you climb over, or down from, when this was more like a landing we had gathered on. After a while my mother stopped murmuring their names and became silent. My father took refuge in paddocks and machinery, kept repeating that a farm won't wait for you and he had a farm to run.

Noel needed to leave, but for too long couldn't bear to go because it seemed to mean abandoning Margaret. For the same reason, we needed him to leave, but couldn't bear to see him go. After a while Martin and Noel could not be in the same room together. At night, Martin drank beer, Noel smoked dope. It became a contest.

I was little help, escaping in whatever way I could, even refusing to attend my graduation, only narrowly achieved. Eventually, defiantly, I cashed in an insurance policy my grandmother had started for me when I was born and bought a ticket to Delhi. I only announced my plans at all because to get a visa into India then a woman was required to have a male relative's signature – her husband, her father, her brother, her uncle, any male relative would do.

'I don't have a husband,' I snapped at the travel agent. Then, thinking of Ross, asked, 'What about a boyfriend?' This would not be stretching the truth too far, surely.

Boyfriend would not do, however. The travel agent curled her lip strenuously and instructed me in immigration law, one of many conversations that would make me a feminist one day. Cowed by my fury, my father signed in the end. He knew why I wanted to leave.

You become accustomed to grief, but for a while I was speeding through a plume of sorrow. Somewhere between Point Peron and Garden Island, I was sitting in the prow of a runabout, ballast, leaning into spray to weigh the boat into the choppy sea. Rottnest was doing its tricks along the horizon's blurry edge: stretching, breaking itself up, melting white, purple and blue streaks between sea and sky.

A hydrogeology course had Ross researching aquifers among the seagrasses of Cockburn Sound, but he kept rescuing me. I had begun disintegrating into nightmares, was on Valium, not coping, might have become a danger to myself… In the grief engulfing my family there was so much rage I could no longer bear to be at home. We had become a family with gaping holes where there used to be safe untidy mesh, and lately each of us had begun falling through in our own way.

The passage to Garden Island can be rough. The boat slapped the sea under me and I gripped its sides. Now and then Ross would dive away like a seal to check the seabed while I drifted alone on the surface, cold hands, salt in my nostrils, islands to contemplate and turn into metaphors of loss, mixed and otherwise. I thrust my weight into westerly winds and felt myself pulled back into wellbeing by a few island-centred weeks in Ross's company.

I could never have imagined then a day arriving decades hence when Ross and I would sit beside Lake Thetis to ponder the meaning of life all over again, that a time would have come when our connection to each other was this irrevocable fact that never seems quite self-evident and yet seems absolutely so, always, no matter how far apart we need to be.

So I turn to him beside the lake this day and say 'Love you', and he leans across and kisses me – no delaying tactics now – and picks up the conversation where we left it.

'Well, I think we should take the Calgary offer, but only if you think you'll cope. You know, in some strange way I can think of him as still being there. Crazy.'

'Not at all,' I interrupt. 'The place belongs to him. I'd love to go back there for a while *because* of him.'

'Well, if you're not happy, we pull the plug. As long as that's the deal, okay?' He looks at me carefully. 'Okay?'

'There'll be stray thoughts, but they're with us wherever we are, like our kidneys or something. Look, just relax, will you? I'll throw myself into projects, be wildly creative...'

He doesn't smile.

'You need to lighten up,' I tell him.

'I'm not sure a person can decide to be happy, that's all.'

'But that applies to you too.'

'Yes, but I'll have work, people who expect me, who expect me in a couple of weeks in fact, if we're going.'

'It won't be the same effort this time, with just the two of us to think about. Anyway, I have *work.*'

On the way back to the motel I announce a whim. 'Maybe I can do something with that turtle shell, you know? Georgia O'Keeffe used skulls, bones, the detritus of death,' I tell Ross. 'Why not? Remember the coral and turquoise mosaics the ancient Mexicans overlaid on the skulls of their dead? We saw them in the British Museum. Mixtec, I think. Art as a form of resurrection, or at least something endured that otherwise couldn't have. It's a kind of treasuring...'

My mind's eye is trained on a skull under glass whose forehead, eyes and nose were all art, while the mouth, with its crooked teeth, was manifestly human. *Why should bones not be a structure upon which a beautiful surface is constructed*, I ask myself, envisaging the shell glazed and its markings polished like fine timber.

'The real tragedy of that turtle's shell would be to waste it,' I say.

Some part of me has begun hanging on, wanting to postpone loss. Or perhaps the impulse to harvest the turtle's shell signals a brief, misguided attempt to take something with me. The more aware I become of another disruption ahead, the more a desire to achieve something despite it is becoming like a disturbance in the air around me.

'I'd like to go down to the beach after dinner anyway, take a look.' Tiny turquoise rectangles drift in my imagination, or is it memory.

'Okay, turtle shell! We'll check it out,' Ross says, willing right now to go along with anything.

Only weeks have elapsed since we drove up to make those farewells. On the way in from the main road a white horse raced us along a paddock fence. Under cloud stretching along the horizon it looked as if it had galloped out of a myth. Sky and landscape seemed to be billowing in unison.

Don't look back, they say, an injunction I have never understood, not even while brushing up against remembered hurdles, detours, sorrows. There are marvels behind. Looking back is one thing, however, and coming back is another. The choice was simple, finally, but as we drove back to the motel that evening I was furiously reassuring myself, as I am now, that I could do all this turning around.

I can. I am neither salt nor stone.

Two

This memoir that sprawls and dashes about all over the place, that wants to be given its head…Writing this, I'm a bareback rider standing astride two galloping steeds: memory and desire – Michèle Roberts

My Dubai is little more than time spent walking, fretting, sitting, thinking, walking. I was ignorant of the hyper-commercial place I read about now, which suggests I barely touched down. Then, it was a redemptive change; now, it is time spent there.

Major restructuring has occurred; departments have merged; positions have been dissolved. My contract will not be renewed.

'Pity,' a colleague says sympathetically. 'They took your best years.' Perhaps he thinks he is helping by making certain I understand the whole business as a savage setback, which until this moment I have not.

In the past when a course peters out, as they do; or is underfunded, as they more often seem to be; or an art department is swallowed or otherwise made to vanish; or contracts are not renewed for reasons that seem increasingly irrational as this thing called economic rationalism takes hold and requires profit-making in education, medicine, prisons, creating troubling vested interests, shrinking that sense of social value that used to buffer us all, I would go home and spend the days gluing shards of porcelain onto old furniture to transform found objects into something I hope to call art, and which happily I have been more and more often able to sell. I know what it is to have the weeks change shape constantly with multiple twists and turns, and because Ross does provide, I know I am free to relish this. I try to honour his tenacity by spending time well in my shed studio. I gave up on the straight line through long ago, see it is far too late for that now.

All easier said than done, of course, all the lived minutes, hours and days of it more intricate and meaningful than retrospection can convey, and all pouring into the river of weeks, months, years meandering behind us now, the life-stream. And this time those incisive words stay with me, making me feel stifled. I just cannot summon up my usual resilience.

Ross tries to kickstart me. 'Come,' he insists. 'It's too hot to do much there right now, but the hotel is part of a vast shopping centre with coffee shops, bookstores. You can keep cool, spend as much time as you like reading, in a luxurious room all to yourself. You always say you want more time for these things. At night we can be tourists, and I could take a couple of days off at the end of the job so we can do some sightseeing. Go further out maybe. Blokes up there call it wadi-bashing, driving in the desert, camping under the stars...'

'You'd love it, Lili. Persia everywhere, in everything, even the most contemporary architecture is marked with it, sky-scrapers with touches of mosque. Mosaic heaven, honestly.'

'Food, culture, desert. You don't know what you're missing...'

'Come on, Lilith, you love to travel...'

Ross, hoisting me back up into a sense of possibility. In the end I gave in, little knowing how grateful I would be one day for modest first-hand memories. In my thoughts Dubai is real at least: it has skin, air, smells, tastes, colour. Being there was a watershed. While I took on the job of defining for myself my best years, Dubai took up residence inside me as a place rather than a word.

Journal fragments, Dubai

The age of the superficial smile. I feel trapped in the jaws of a compulsory grin. I've been reading about how depression is what we do to recoup, a chemical change in response to a hostile environment, a safety mechanism that causes us to withdraw, rest, recuperate, a human wound-licking procedure. So this misery is nothing more than being a human being in Dubai...

Blood from generations back threads its way through me and moves on, or will if Kate and Nan have children, a point on which I must keep room for doubt since our daughters are talented, ambitious, mobile girls. Sometimes I fear that river of blood coming to an end inside my veins, imagine myself having been here only to have been, no mark in the sand. We ought to be satisfied, in fact there's no choice, but perhaps there is such a thing as biological panic...

I suppose I'll look for another job. It should be simple enough except for questions of age and damage – damnage. Or I'll end up talking to myself about going with the flow, as usual, fine fatalistic sentiments only possible because of Ross, whose submissions are so much larger. Once again everything depends on him…

A lost in Dubai day, a day lost in Dubai. Hot and dry. Queer how places we remember vividly are often where we were unhappy or uncomfortable, as if misery seals them in. I ought to remember this room, then; bleakness has me by the throat here. I know people triumph over more painful adjustments than any I'm facing, but right now contentment seems like some dream state and the woman I thought I was is slipping away…

I am working my eyes to the edge of a table. Soon I'll find the courage to look past it in the other direction, down this multi-layered corridor of shops stretching endlessly away. How can I have been so insulated that I feel nervous and lost in a coffee shop as ordinary as Miss Maud's in Fremantle? Except the floor under my feet is exquisitely tiled, and at the Armenian Trading Company opposite, rugs in great splatterings of colour and design are like great messy flower gardens announcing Persia.

Only three other tables are occupied. At one, the man who runs this coffee shop sits looking bored. At another, two young white-robed sheikhs are yelling into mobile phones in Arabic, mellifluous but bellowed, as they make call after call. At the third, a man and wife sit in silence. She has just uncovered her face and we exchanged smiles when she caught me looking at her curiously, or I caught her looking at me curiously. I'm glad to have received a smile that is usually veiled, and grateful for her small kindness.

Down the mall the sign City Centre Hotel beckons, my sense of Sofitel security. I write in my journal while I sit here because I feel conspicuous and am aware of my difference, dislike being noticed as intensely as I dislike being photographed, except sometimes by Ross when I don't have time to think about it.

If this were a photograph you'd see a coffee cup, a muffin paper, half a butter pat, seven sugar packets, two small jars of jam, a sprig of maidenhair fern in a small white vase. And me.

The fern is real. The men in their flowing robes are real. The woman in black robes is real. Piped music in the background: 'on the street where you live...' seems utterly unreal...

In our cool green room I feel cast adrift, lost in its great space, want to take it in, want to believe Ross that what lies ahead is pure opportunity. His efforts to buoy me up can be more infuriating than up-buoying, and his hopes for me often feel like expectations. But he makes me feel loved, which is more important than the fear that I'm probably extinguished as a teacher of art and art history and whatever else it is that I have been doing. Perhaps I'll become the artist I've only ever flirted with becoming.

'Amateur' after all, is *amatore* in Italian, from Latin *amator* 'lover', or from *amare* 'to love'...

Facing facts in a window filled with white, hot light. It's forty-eight degrees outside. Buildings float in heat, seem insubstantial. Numbers appear electronically above the tennis courts I look down on through vast window panes. No one has played on them since we've been here. They are green rectangles, just out there, baking…

Kate and Nan used to call my mosaics Mum's shard labour. Perhaps there's a solution in their little joke, something to give me a new sense of direction – I will throw myself into reverse…

Such heat shrivels your lungs. How anyone can work in it is beyond me, but this afternoon I have watched bare-chested men lugging huge chunks of limestone off a truck to make the border of a new garden, tattered men who are no doubt very poor. I watched them stop to kneel and pray among the rocks they were unloading, just one of the different behaviours we all take absolutely for granted, depending who we are, this one fascinating to me, ordinary to them.

The soil for the new garden beds is trucked in from Saudi Arabia, an effort so extreme I can't help wondering why they do it when this wide white beauty is its own kind of perfection. Surely things were not meant to be green everywhere…

I used to be thrilled by the anonymity a journey brings, that sense of being cut loose. I can settle for being a receiver of sights again, an antenna for the unfamiliar, for what things might mean. Something is surfacing, a feeling of renewal…

In the lift today I realised how everything I've ever seen of an Arab family has been lined with the invisible.

What does it mean that I've never had access to the reality of the fine light texture of white fabric with which men cover their heads? Or that the black cord holding it in place is so glossy and fine, and the stitching on a dishdasha is tough like the stitching on a pair of jeans?

The physical presence of a culture I've only seen in images is a battery of small shocks and I'm struck by what we can never hope to know about each other, so should never presume to think we do know. Films and news reports have turned the world into a crude contest that robs it of reality and saps its strength, all the images facile and empty. I want to touch everything, fill myself up with the unfamiliar real…

The mall is all hard surfaces like huge malls anywhere, only bigger. And cool, wonderfully cool. So I started from the large marbled hall at the entrance to the arcade and it took me all afternoon to make my way through. The comfortable invisibility of walking down a familiar street was a long way off. I am either stared at or targeted with a studied hostile indifference. Both make me self-conscious and uncomfortable.

By contrast, a pair of blonde girls clipped past me at one point, wearing skimpy tops and hipster skirts – bare legs, bouncing breasts on display. It seems outrageous to dress like that here. Silly girls. They confuse aggression with freedom and insensitivity with self-expression.

American sailors wander in twos and threes, exactly like in Fremantle and Northbridge, only here their demeanour is somehow sinister, especially because they can't contain their curiosity about the women in black abayas. In the face of that sense of permission, no wonder the women of Dubai hold those veils so firmly together. Perhaps young blonde girls bare their bodies needily, to draw soldierly attention away from all those dark eyes.

As I watch these sailors, who are every bit as fascinating as the women they watch, it seems their triangular bodies with thick necks and all that worked-on muscle, all that strutting and carefully trained aggression, are floating around the world just waiting for something to happen, making it happen.

We're supposed to believe they keep things safe, but I notice how discourteous they feel free to be here. None of the 'Excuse me, ma'ams' we get at home or see in movies. There is more aggression, more soldier than we see in Fremantle when a ship is in, or is it just a different generation and training can't contain such men inside old-fashioned courtesies any more? They push and shove people aside, barge to the fronts of queues, fill up aisles with their dangerous-toy bodies and belligerently refuse to move aside to let locals pass. They set out to make it clear they do not like Arabs, these boys – and most of them are only that – exhibit deliberate contempt for this culture just because it is other than their own. They behave as though they are in untrustworthy territory, and for them perhaps it is, but as far as I can see tension in the mall begins with their presumptuous stares. All the peaks of their baseball caps are reversed, a sign of how impressionable they are, how unthinking. They look like swollen children, stupid and belligerent. I do not feel the world is safe in their hands…

Most of today went on a search for a book about the desert tombs Ross and I saw in the museum last night. One skeleton was of a man from 3,000 BC, buried in a cairn holding a small clay cup to his lips.

Among bodies excavated from the tombs of Qatar and Jabel Hafit were a husband and wife buried three millennia ago holding hands and with legs entwined. We speculated about their deaths, whether she was killed to be with him.

We suppose it to be such a dreadful thought, but I do see how the idea of living on alone could be worse, how for some companions it might seem sensible and not terror-filled at all, just a setting out together and a question of faith. They are profoundly comforting in some way, this couple, with a kind of timelessness in their embrace. People from a life that in the blink of a cosmic eye was gone, and yet they hold each other these five thousand years later. I hope it was an accident, or a pact, but if not, I see how she might not have been afraid.

The skeleton of the man clutching his cup seems solitary, and tragic for it. Flesh-and-blood hands would have pressed his small clay cup into shape and put it on the side of a well to dry in the sun. It would have been passed from one person to another until it reached whoever had the task of winding his lifeless fingers around it and setting him on his path. Such a ritual no doubt had something to do with water…

It hasn't rained in Dubai for more than a year. The waiter serving me lunch today said, 'Madam, the water has died'...

I went back to the museum. In the bones of long-dead people I glimpse the life in death, still have moments of regret that my memory jammed there for so long. After all, the girls' births are the two glowing events in our own past, which seems as busy as the Milky Way from here, and now there are countless more happy than unhappy memories. Maybe some recoveries go on to the very end...

I want to know where the original tombs are, feel a kind of grief about the removal of the dead they yield for the likes of me to contemplate. I'm reminded of the Batavia boy in the maritime museum in Fremantle, dug out of Abrolhos Island sand and transported down the coast to be laid out like a jigsaw in a display case, lit up for us to peer at missing chunks in his skull and shoulder, scars left by a mutineer's axe. I like to imagine he died for refusing to participate in that killing spree. I've gazed at him often enough, thinking about the fact that he was some mother's child. Apparently DNA tests on his bones have revealed he was about twenty-one.

About the age our son would have been...

Flicking through this notebook now, a record of my brief stay in Dubai, I fetch up here, reminded of another skeleton I stood beside once, in the British Museum, feeling apologetic there too towards whoever it used to be. I was looking for ancient Mexican mosaics, but I was compelled to eavesdrop when a father called his child over, not only because I notice little boys, but in this case because of a coincidence – we had given our son the same name.

'Look, a dead person, mate,' the father said, forcing the child to take notice of that foetal cluster of bones.

He was all eyes. 'Is it someone, Dad? A real human?'

That was a father dedicated to the idea of toughening up, the sort of man who dunks a child he's teaching to swim under and under, until he has no breath left for crying. Ross's fathering has been conscientious and gentle, and it seems sad that his kind of manhood will never be passed from father to son. Such thoughts sneak up on me safely these days, are more a question of noticing than grieving.

Kate and Nan love their father without complication. I think of him at their births. His hands, how he held me, let go when I couldn't bear to be touched, wanting to do whatever I wanted of him, helplessness, fear, awe in his eyes – I discovered then that these are more than mere abstractions.

And then last time, his generosity and courage. Perhaps intimacy with a man's tears will make a woman's love irrevocable.

At this distance the experience of birth seems to belong to someone else, as if that astonishingly naked woman could never have been me. The doctors were right. We do forget pain. What they never mention is the time it takes for the memory to fade, or the holes it leaves in its wake. They don't seem to know about these.

I see myself at the first birth, ringing the night bell, Ross pushing at the hospital door, recall the shock of love that was unleashed when I had Kate, the very fact of her existence. Then I see myself arriving at the hospital in labour with Nan three years later, knowing what lay ahead this time, my fervent reluctance, the moment of truly comprehending inevitability.

Each time, just a few hours later, a baby girl. Such a small accumulation of lived minutes, and they contained the core of time.

Journal fragments, Dubai

The only books I can find are about English explorers and scholars, the Lawrence of Arabia syndrome. I don't want nineteenth-century imperial adventures. Truth be known, I'm looking for the words of scholars who can tell me everything...

Moods as blotchy as my skin. The colour draining from my hair. Feeling no longer whole. I stall in front of mirrors, find myself taking stock, self-absorption that has more to do with having lost my sense of completeness than vanity.

Menopausal. I realise now I've heard the word spoken mostly with derision at its edges, but I also believed the tales, that it would be a time of surging energy, that I'd feel strong and free. Instead, positive thought seems delusional and I find myself lamenting my age despite everything I intended to feel.

A body never just is; from birth to death we're in a state of change, I know, but that knowledge isn't helping as I become this diminished woman. I feel kinship with self-destructing salmon swimming upstream to their

spawning grounds, am shocked to be making such a
comparison, find myself making it nonetheless, seem to
be experiencing everything transformative as damage…

Life is turning out to be constant fission, identities
peeling away. So another me lately consigned to the
past, but because of it I'm free to enjoy this splendid
air-conditioned Dubai hotel instead of preparing for a
round of struggles over courses, funding, the incessant
whisper of territorial rights up and down the corridors.
Because of Ross, I sit in a window overlooking what
feels like another world, while he moves in and out
of air-conditioned relief in some yard. And because
he's willing to work in forty-eight degrees Celsius, we
don't depend on my salary. And because of him I sit in
comfort writing this.

   This morning he said he wants me to resist becoming
one of those people whose disappointments take up
residence in their eyes…

I've seen the downfall of other marriages, perhaps
that's the thing. I know no one is immune, that to
believe Ross and I would be is simply stupid. I fear new
possibilities in his head, want the clasped hands for the
thousand years, us safely and irrevocably entwined, all
the implications of age with our gaze full-on, for them
never to matter in that cheap, appraising, mean-spirited
way, for us to be able to love each other exactly as we are.
   I could never have understood any of this when I
was young, so perhaps there is a shift towards wisdom,
perhaps forever means love in the present tense…

The bookshop turns out to be crammed with books on trade. The United Arab Emirates come across primarily as a capitalist success story, an investment in the future, a venture of money rather than soul. The best I've been able to find on the tombs is a paragraph in a guidebook and a couple of postcards.

A suspicious young man followed me up and down aisles today. I'm not used to being regarded as a potential thief. Then at the cash register an American sailor pushed to the front and shoved a greeting card covered in red roses across the counter. It read: *A message of love from Dubai.* Of course he was served ahead of everyone else; the young cashier had no choice. Shared resentment passed up and down the line and eye contact divided around me and I saw myself regarded as one of Them...

Today took me down an arcade of designer dress shops where I saw a hot-pink concoction costing thousands of American dollars, a dress I cannot imagine wanting to own, or wear, but it reignited my lament for lost youth. My reflection floating pinkly in the window reminded me of Ross's story about a sighing fish...

Today I've spent hours staring down on the cream and beige rooftops below this window, an Escher world of ladders, air-conditioning towers, skylights, all with a compelling Persian note. On one wall the word Emirates is cut in half so it only reads *rates.* Another building has Ikea emblazoned on it but, wonderfully to my eye, in blue and yellow Arabic...

I must go out despite the heat, can't stay cooped up like this. Although the Arabs do. My Dubai memories will be sparsely populated. Dubai, on the edges of which I can barely say I have a toehold, a Dubai that will have been hotel room, cavernous mall, bookshop, café, museum, set against white expanses passed through at high speeds, or not at all, but how vivid it is to be here…

I don't want this to be just another place I pass through with all the old memories, dissatisfactions, my husk-self intact, want to let go, be able to imagine life so far as something elemental, part of a dust cloud being tossed across white space by a wind, leaving behind countless fragments of possibility in its wake. How wonderful to think the wind here really does carry in it all the perfumes of Arabia…

Incredibly, the new millennium is upon us and we'll be home by New Year's Eve, but Kate and Nan will already have left. How frustrating to be missing them by just a couple of weeks. The condition of the empty nest, I guess. Kate tells us she has tried on our behalf, but all the restaurants in Perth are booked out, so not even a special dinner is likely.

I imagined I'd be prancing about in high heels when this New Year came, would be kissing my way through the turn, aloft, vibrant, wildly alive and rejoicing. Instead our change of millennium promises to slip quietly in and quietly out.

Although not as quietly as the next, by which time we'll have been clutching our dry little cups for the thousand years...

Noticing is a form of event. Dubai is reminding me of the Lilliputian facts of life, with its offerings of tiny intersections and path-crossings, emptying self-pity out of me like the swill it is. A lot can happen within the walls of a hotel room. Mine will have been domestic adventures, a life lived out among the details, the overlooked, the minutiae. Another life is pressing at me from this sliver of contemporary Arabia. Possibilities begin to have something to do with concentrating on art of my own instead of coaching and coaxing others. From today I will make fruitfulness mean some other thing...

There's plenty to discover going up and down in a lift, or walking the glossy corridors of a hotel or mall. Tonight a girl about Nan's age shared the lift with us. Her black abaya was open and underneath she was wearing the hot-pink dress from the arcade. A glittering necklace followed its plunging neckline down between her breasts. She must have been the most expensively dressed woman I have ever seen, and certainly one of the most beautiful. She pursed her lips into the lift's mirrored walls, applying mulberry lipstick, fluffing her hair, ostentatiously making of us dust mites, exercising the deliberate invisibility we inflict upon those we choose not to see or be seen by. Just before the doors opened onto the world that matters, she clipped her black veil together and the splendour disappeared. She walked away clenching fabric over the lower half of her face, from where it fell straight to the ground, weighed down by black sequins at the hem, a disappearing act of her own volition, an eclipse.

We agreed that her mother had absolutely no idea where she was, that she was off to be bad. Then we spent most of dinner conjecturing about what Kate and Nan might be up to – Katie off to Tasmania in search of wilderness, Nan well and truly back in India by the time we get home. We miss them more than we can tell even each other, and sometimes the point we have reached in life feels like disintegration, new kinds of separateness producing this vacuum at the centre of my world...

Seeing worlds is to be alive, to let myself wholly *be* in this blink of an eye – which is all, after all – to let myself be this woman in this skin, only that.

Although I don't know what she could have to say about anything except what it was like to be a moderately prosperous, moderately wounded, moderately hung-up and confused, blessedly well-loved Australian woman at the end of the second millennium. Perhaps it will be enough, before I curl up around the human being I've lived it with and go to sleep for good...

You can actually see the heat outside today. In the hills, only a day's drive away, is the tomb of Job. You are in the Arabian Desert, Lilith. The dunes are rippled by wind. This is the country of the Bedou, and today seems like the source of all that was ever hot and dry in the world. Take it in. Let go. Let be. Cut the present tense loose, let it drift, be *in* it...

By that night in Cervantes, Ross and I knew the tangle of memory we were climbing along was unlikely to lead back to Dubai, but experience was hovering over our choice. This would be an opportunity to live there that would never come again. I had been told that in Dubai I would need Ross's written permission to drive, open a bank account, all that, but such things were beginning to matter less. At the same time the other trajectory, the one that brings us back to Calgary, was sketching itself in.

Journal fragment, Cervantes

So many impossibilities construct the boundaries of our lives. Impossible to read every book you want to, or to live in all the beckoning places: island, houseboat, warehouse, city loft, castle, skyscraper, monastery, hermitage, whitewashed cottage...Life is a series of improvisations, and it is turning out to be just too small for all of them...

Trudging down the beach in moonlight, we are still discussing our new prospects when Ross, the pragmatic one, drops his toolbox on the sand. He is irritable: 'Why in god's name are we doing this, Lil? It'll stink the car out and you won't have time to do anything with it before we go. It's not only illegal, it's ridiculous!'

'Insane,' I say, and we end up slumped against each other on the beach in the dark laughing. 'Just an idea,' I say.

The end of uncertainty. Staring into noisy darkness where the sea is, I am glad to be relieved of the prospect of butchering a turtle. I console myself by trying to imagine it whole, a humped swimmer in a turquoise ocean just going about its business when something happens, something out of the blue.

Later, propped up in bed reading about Chekhov, I come across an anecdote. Writing about himself appalled him so deeply that when he was asked for a biography he would write a mock version. It reads like chastisement to a woman with a journal on her bedside table, brings on another deluge of self-doubt, so I falter in whatever this is by which I track our progress. Nevertheless, I make an entry in my notebook before turning off the lamp – ritual, habit of a lifetime, mild obsessiveness, fear of being unable to sleep if I don't empty my mind – but because of Chekhov I write only briefly.

Journal fragment, Cervantes
I spin a life with my few daily words. I'm writing these in Cervantes, here to decide, to say goodbye. How unpredictable life is. We may be on our way back to Calgary in less than a month. The time has come to ring Kate and Nan, let them know what's in the wind…

I sense Ross staring into the dark. 'It's not called a book of changes for nothing I suppose,' he jokes. 'Maybe we should throw that Ching. Can't hurt.'

'Seems like an appropriate question to ask of the ineffable, you think? Whither next?'

'No doubt it'll tell us what the wise man would have done,' he laughs.

Ross is nothing if not tenacious. There is determination in his voice. He rolls over and I curl myself around him.

Our copy of the *I Ching* has an introduction by Carl Jung, which surely means something sensible. The leather-bound volume is a whimsy belonging to a friendship I look back on fondly, a gift. I go to sleep wondering where that friend, Colleen, is these days, and musing about how opting for a road already taken is to take the one not taken in the poem. The paradox charms me into submission every time. *Life loops with good reason*, I tell myself, looking for peace of mind.

Peace of mind arrives in a dream. I am bathing a baby boy in a small porcelain coracle. I cup his tiny head in one hand and with the other I am squeezing water out of a sponge so it rains on him. His eyes are wide in that way babies have of looking at the world, so hugely they seem to be letting it all in at once. He wriggles, tries to swivel, twists face down in the water. Drops caught in his eyelashes make his expression seem utterly familiar, as though I have done this with him many times.

Then I am carrying him as only an infant can be carried, with his head cupped in my hand and his body stretched along my forearm like an offering. His tiny feet kick against my chest. He is watching me. Our eyes are locked. Babies do this, hook your gaze as firmly as if they had cast a line into you. They can hold you for as long as they like with their planetary eyes. This gaze is an exchange of souls. It flows between beings who are mother and son.

Then I am carrying him along a wide light corridor, the walls of which form a tunnel through a vast aquarium. The light is aquamarine, the like of which I have never actually seen, a distillation of blue, essence of what I imagine the celestial to be. Fish school near the glass and dart away, massed flickers of all that is gorgeous, a speeding rainbow sometimes, a marine palette at others. My son and I are passing through colour itself.

We walk on through intense turquoise translucence until I sense we are being visited, and out of horizontal blue depths a great ray swims slowly into view. For a while it contemplates us with a profoundly comforting gaze, like being regarded with affection by someone you love. Eventually, huge wings undulating, it turns and disappears into the blue, as if satisfied of delivering its message.

Dreams draw no conclusions, and in this one we just keep walking into wakefulness, where I can hardly bear to find I have left the place we were in and he is not in my arms after all, and that mine are not the young, firm arms and hands of the dream mother. It seemed to be a vision of all that is uterine, and so vivid it lodges in my heart. A reality of sorts, then.

I lie there awake, eyes closed, feeling a deep restfulness for the first time since his small life, it seems. And with something in it of forgiving myself, of learning all over again that serenity is not a question of forgetting or of leaving behind, but a matter of learning to live with the losses instead of against them.

I decide not to share this dream with Ross until I can tell it without tears. It is comfort enough to have decided for myself that I should look for contentment in this journey backwards. My Pisces son has reassured me.

I hold that thought close while I pull the bedcovers over my head and begin musing about how my heart is always trailing behind somewhere, usually looking for Kate and Nan these days, and about how I will fit our family into the convoluted process by which we are about to be caught up in the expatriate tide again. Sleep reclaims the morning, and half-remembering, half-dreaming, flittering, I am soon putting together one of my earliest exhibitions again. I am unpacking mosaic bowls, only this time surrounded by pompous men making remarks about being serious artists and only here to encourage their bored and disappointed wives who, having finished childbearing and -rearing, find themselves at loose ends and have taken up painting, collage, pottery, whatever it is I do.

A man with a silver ponytail and an embroidered jacket looks Ross up and down and asks, 'What about you, Ross? You look pretty much nine-to-five to me. What are you doing here?'

'Helping Lilith out,' Ross says, without irony.

What Ross looks, is exhausted. To make it in time to help me set up, he has left home at five that morning and has come straight from the office. I see him spot the condescension, let it crackle in the air and burn itself out while he takes off his jacket and tie.

'Ross is a fantastic photographer,' I say, making it worse.

Ross could be one of those men in John Brack's painting, *Five o'clock Collins Street*, suit-wearing men supposed to be indistinguishable from each other. He could be the man

96

third from the left, say, and on his way to the car park, hoping that just this once he can get out quickly. Waiting in city traffic has become deadly and augments a whole day of inhaling downtown air. He is more than tired this day; he is exhausted, and depressed.

It could be the day he came down in the lift with a man from the twenty-fifth floor, also in suit and tie and carrying a briefcase, but with tears running down his face and speaking to no one in particular. 'Christ, I hate my job! I've just had to fire seventy-four people. Think of it!'

'I didn't know what to do,' Ross told me, misery etched in his face. 'I waited in the lobby, but he refused to get out, kept his back to the corner avoiding his reflection, riding up and down. He was trying to recover, I guess. I said I was sorry about his situation and left him to it, because that's what I thought he wanted me to do.'

That happened on the kind of dull, wintry day I detect in Brack's painting. Ross has always suffered when the weather goes on and on being grey. Sometimes the pathetic fallacy is lived experience.

Or it could have been the night after the fish had sighed in Dubai. Ross was fending off his weariness of consulting, conferencing, networking, was sick of making the best of things, felt he'd lost sight of whatever it is you work for, towards, the thing that keeps you going.

'Just tired, dog-tired,' he told me, calling home after-wards. It was one of the few times he wished aloud that he could do something else. He said he hated meals in hotels and restaurants, hated functions, being always away. He had been thinking about walking out on this business dinner and catching the next flight home when he noticed a groper settling carefully into the chipped marble bed of an aquarium beside him.

'I was sitting there trying not to give a damn and it looked straight at me. And it sighed,' he said. 'I swear to you, Lili, it sighed. As if it knew something, or wanted me to know something.'

My imagined fish of his story has always been a slick, muscular being with an artist's eye, appraising Ross through the glass, seeing a man tired, lonely, not in the mood. And of course the fish is not in the mood for dying. Mutual sadness fuses them.

'I looked into its eyes and it nearly had me in tears. Christ, I think I'm burning out,' Ross said on the phone.

I resorted to jokes. 'You'd better be careful about eye contact, Ross. Don't want you turning into a groper.' I told him about Julio Cortázar's story about a man and an axolotl.

'The thing about an axolotl,' he said, turning my attempt at humour aside, 'is that they're nearly blind, but this fish could see me. It looked straight at me. It wanted me to know it knew something.'

His strange fish story has stayed with me, how to its eye all those faces must have looked the same. The fact is Ross is often exhausted. And because we have ended up as we appear to be ending up, I can see no way of relieving him of the burden. Not that I consoled him then, either. He was too far away.

It was one of many times when I have been an insufficient wife, I think now, looking back. I fantasise that the fish perhaps recognised in one man's deep weariness the weariness of all overworked human beings who are supposed to interpret their situation as privilege. I decide our kind of life is misrepresented in Brack's painting. It meanly misses the spirit of putting one foot before the other, stolidly, hopefully, one day after the other, for a lifetime. The optimism, generosity and concentration of such a life are nowhere to be found. Dedication is missing. The painting lacks compassion, I decide. And the self-important husbands lack insight.

All this mattered that morning, because in my half-sleep people like us are the subjects of Brack's painting. I have become one of the wives waiting at home beyond the picture. Ross would put one foot before the other along that grey street, feeling the artist's smug derision as though there is a choice, when from street to street it is only the nature of the uniform that changes. He would make his way home through the crowds to me and I would be waiting, invisibly, beyond the frame, a Penelope-fact my mother took for granted and that I have resisted all my life.

My mother's voice arrives from long ago. 'At least with teaching, Lilith, you'll always have something to fall back on.'

Instead I fall back on this *art business*, as she called it, and which she saw as a distraction from the life she imagined for me. Have had to, have to, am having to, and it has taken this long to discern the pleasures of that falling-back. No more excuses. No time. In my mother's remembered voice I hear the rumble of the falls.

I make a promise to myself that from now on I will imagine Ross and me as Klimt's golden, patchwork-quilted lovers instead. If I must imagine us dead, let it be with legs entwined under a gorgeous coverlet, suspended in a gleaming mosaicised kiss. Such imaginings as can make the 'Death do us part' part – always the down side of merged lives – less shattering.

When Ross kisses me on the forehead this particular morning, I jump into wakefulness.

'Hey, you,' he says. 'Get a move on. We have to check out in less than half an hour.'

'I wish we'd gone to that restaurant in Dubai. You know…'

As if we inhabit the same mind or live in a single ongoing conversation, he knows immediately. 'That was the first time, not when you came. One thing's for sure, that poor fish is nothing but a dim memory,' he says. After a pause he adds, 'You've got no idea what a relief it is that you went when you did. This decision's way too important not to be mutual.'

'Anyway, I really do think Calgary,' I say.

He turns. 'I thought we settled it last night.'

'It's settled.'

'Second thoughts?'

'None.'

'Why don't I believe you?'

'We'll have to rent out the house. I'll call an agent tomorrow, start packing up the studio. We can do this.'

Even the shaving circle Ross has wiped onto the mirror is blank. The bathroom is so steam-filled, entering it has the quality of a disappearing act.

A couple of days later, helping Ross pack up his office, I am shocked to see him remove an image from a nearby wall, admittedly a cruel photograph of a naked woman with a bag on her head and astonishing to find there at all in this day and age my daughters call post-feminist. He folds the poster with precise destructiveness and stuffs it with uncharacteristic venom into a car park bin on our way out.

'Ethical activism,' he says to my enquiry. 'Or activist ethics. A social intervention anyway. He'll never know, and if he does, let him, silly bugger. I'm a father of daughters, for god's sake…'

As we drive under the Narrows, light from the renovated brewery floats on the Swan River like a controversial question and reminds me of a ship of lights they used to string up here for Christmas. I ponder how all this will sit here reflecting, floating, hardly altering while we go and live out a piece of life where people don't know or care that this place even exists.

'Nearly done,' I say. 'Less than a week to go.'

'I've started looking forward to it. By today I was achieving exactly nothing.'

He means at work. To avoid thinking about achievement, a word to which I am sensitive again, I sort through the mental list of what I had hoped to fit in before departure date – visit the art gallery to see the Impressionist exhibition, make a last trip to Rottnest, have lunch with friends…

My reverie stalls when Ross says, 'Funny how you suddenly remember things you haven't thought of for years,' and launches into a story about camping once on a dry white lake teeming with spiders like tiny scurrying ghosts.

'Nightmare?' I ask.

'Maybe. Don't think so.'

'How incredible that you've never told me that in all the time we've been together.'

He laughs. 'It just never crossed my mind, I suppose. We're not open books yet are we, Lili?' He adds as an afterthought, 'Do we want to be?'

An appealing insight, that we'll never be each other no matter how long we go on offering each other pieces of the days, building this overlap. Interface. Interlace.

'Dreams can be incredible,' I say. It seems a good time to tell him about mine, but despite my best efforts the tears come.

So, trying not to let Ross know, there I am, weeping my way down Stirling Highway, and not only because the life I am in is ending. Perhaps it was nothing more than a memory of bathing Kate and Nan, except this baby with his wide-eyed expression did not look quite like either of the girls ever looked. I am certain I have never actually seen that particular child at that particular age. I know in my heart he was who he would have been.

Now, placing the Dubai notebook on a glass shelf with others I have lined up there, my attention is drawn to one beside it, filled with quotations, signs of the way travelled along my personal trail of ink. It opens at a quotation I must have copied out more than ten years ago. John Barth, surfacing into the room with what seems like a fair warning: 'In each and any case, so what? One more short or not-so-short story of a bourgeois romance, domestic tribulation, personal and vocational fulfillment or frustration, while the world grinds on.'

'Precisely. Only when you consider it, how miraculous,' I tell the window woman, my voice sounding unnaturally loud in the empty apartment, as if I can no longer find its proper volume.

In our story all the usual memories, hopes and dreams accumulate, a bit like images I put together in my workshop, and these days with reasonably practised eye, I am pleased to remind myself. Despite a hand so damaged that not even pressure on a doorbell brings the results it should, I have persisted with my craft. It has taught me to be intrigued by anything cast off. All fragments have a history.

Turning to a pristine new notebook with the usual childlike feeling of being issued a new pad at school, I take up my pen. It is time to enter the moment I am in.

Journal fragment, Calgary
Tomorrow is my birthday. Life is passing by the decade now. How astonishing to be here, about to be adjusted, added to, tweaked by this oil city again, everything unfamiliar and at the same time oddly familiar. Coming back feels inevitable and like a pilgrimage of sorts, but also like a random change of direction. I want to resist the rug-pulled-out-from-under-me feeling, want to enjoy the sense of having stepped up into this wintry eyrie. The world outside is intensely quiet, as if someone had pressed a mute button, as if the city were empty.

Over the past few days, there have been shop assistants, and I spoke with the two men who delivered these four chairs, table and sofa, holding great weight in the air while they slipped snow-wet shoes off and on with Canadian equanimity. Today the intercom phone rang, a diverting convenience – it was the security desk downstairs calling to confirm that I was expecting Emily. I had to tell them, 'Wrong apartment.' I don't know any Emilys. Not in this country. Not any more.

These security men say goodbye when you leave the building, hello when you come back. I answer with those two words, *Good morning* or *Good afternoon*, hearing my voice. Otherwise, hours and hours, days, pass in silence. We are taking up residence in a high-rise hush.

I'm not sleeping well. It's the middle of the night. I'm sitting in front of a glass wall that is already my favourite place in the apartment. I'd forgotten the perfect geometry of snow-covered roofs and fresh white strips of road, the beauty of snow building up like ice-cream on window sills, comforting rediscoveries while I wait for my circadian rhythms to adjust.

It takes time for an address to feel like home. I've spent today being a hausfrau, arranging and rearranging what little furniture we have yet, tackling a box now and then, unpacking clothes, papers, books, so far.

Reading Anne Carson's *The Beauty of the Husband* feels like flying through a clever storm. Also leafing through old notebooks, of which I should never have brought so many, except I thought they might be inspiration for something I could vaguely imagine doing, although I have no idea yet which room in this apartment I could make my own.

A birthday seems like the perfect time for noticing how slowly life reveals you to yourself. Right now, if

I could wish for anything, it would be that I hadn't wasted so much time. I daresay most people would say the same thing, so I ban self-pity. It's not as if it will be the first solo birthday of my life...

I put down my pen. This is a note to my future, clearly. Words that will one day launch me back into this snow flurry, this beige room, destined as it is to become the setting for my new recent past. I feel caught in a net of light, or a memory web.

Cross-secting my life with places, even places where I have done only tiny bits of living, I can pierce my memory and begin an eruption, at first of pleasure, but invariably a drift towards sadness and nostalgia follows. I usually go to the edge of that sweet crater and dive nevertheless, which now plunges me back into a world of sandstone and sea where subtle blues are inflected by all manner of green, and white beaches glitter in the sun.

I am reaching an age when looking back on beginnings makes a particular kind of sense. In fact, remembering strikes me as a kind of subsidence; certain fragments shove their way to the surface while others are left behind, a bit like islands. A thought predicated just now on a small fact that seems as biological as it is biographical, that when I intersect myself with places today I find Rottnest Island in my bones. Perhaps because it is such a far cry from Calgary in a snowstorm, with its minus-eighteen outside. Or perhaps because at such a distance Rottnest is synonymous with the word *home*. Whatever the reason, that tiny piece of land is tied to my sense of home like a kite.

In the year divers will come across the wreck of the *Cervantes*, everything about home seems in desperate need of being left behind. I am at Rottnest with friends, confusing my deliberate, casual, adolescent waywardness with some vague idea of renewal that is driving me on, away, inward.

As girls on the verge of more enigmatic selves we are likely to be found walking sedately along beaches, unconsciously longing for orchestral music to waft in on a soundtrack wind. We can while away winsome hours of days, of weeks, gazing into blue summer haze as if it could tell us the future. We collect shells, linger in melaleuca groves, feed quokkas, ride around the island to keep ourselves twig-thin, spend whole afternoons at the Basin reading. We are waiting for Heathcliff, believe *Women in Love* says it all, think *all* is always elsewhere.

At night we might be playing Scrabble and Rickety Kate by candlelight, or going to the pub, or hoping for messages from ouija boards, spending tipsy hours comparing childhoods and rapidly becoming people who know too much about each other. We are turning into old friends who try less to please and will soon be more like siblings we need to live apart from, but we don't know it yet.

We are well practised at distinguishing between daytrippers and island people. Daytrippers trail a kind of longing by midday, and their afternoons speed up while ours slow down. When the last ferry leaves, the world is out and we are in. And being in, is Being *In*. Among us, petty elitisms have become an infection. We want to be Discriminating Women of the World. We play Beat the Bourgeois, working with silly approximations – a dislike of kitsch like china ducks flying up walls, dolly toilet-roll covers, doilies, floral carpets, has begun to dominate our social consciousness, as if such trivia mattered. All we manage to achieve are hurt feelings and a growing reluctance to take each other into our mothers' homes.

Being a farmer's daughter I can be relieved that home is too far away to be dropped in on, because at Cervantes there would be no escaping the floral carpets and pretty toilet-seat covers that represent comfort to my mother's mind. I love my mother. I want to protect her from the tongues of my clever friends.

Being university students, we have added our numbers to marches against the Vietnam War, but truth be told the very word *moratorium* excites us as much as anything, and wanting to stop the war does not distract us from decisions about what to wear to a protest. We are not altogether superficial, however, genuinely believing ourselves to be ferocious with desire to change the world; it is just that war is a phenomenon in which we find it hard to believe. Yet.

This time I have flown over. By now we make cottage bookings to fit around summer jobs at pizza parlours, department stores, Power Coaching, factory cleaning. We travel from the mainland independently and make our own way to wherever we are staying rather than disembark from the ferry in a pack. Arriving late and by plane makes me feel groovy and cool – celebrated feelings I do not often enjoy, being a young woman who rattles around inside herself, although hoping by this time that no one hears much noise. Aplomb comes with practice, of which I have not yet had enough, but the island is teaching me to leave home with what my mother calls a good grace.

Always in the singular, always making of grace an indefinite article.

This summer I will discover that being kissed is not the same as kissing. In the sand dunes in the rain, I am kissed by a boy with a pretty face. I am more casual by now about passionate kisses, even from strangers like him, can make cool judgements about a thing called performance, have friends whose jokes, like 'Sam, the ceiling needs painting', and quotes, like 'Think of England', make them seem positively sophisticated. They are teaching me a thing or two, friends. In the sandhills that night I am tempted to lose my virginity, but it turns out I have the fear of god in me yet. We all still make fine distinctions between Petting, Heavy Petting, Going All The Way.

I try to imagine this language in my daughters' mouths now. Kate would choke on her double espresso with hot milk on the side. Nan would look sad for me. I am their mother; I know their emancipations are real.

The thing is, Rottnest then was a place where you could *become*. For those of us who grew up on the coast where Penguin Island, Garden Island, Carnac and Rottnest float off the west in bits, there was always something about walking across names etched into rocks like a roll call, something about rocks like great bookends, and the sash of mainland lights across the dark, and the uterine sound of the sea on a warm night, some romantic thing about Rotto. The nineteen kilometres of Gage Roads between Perth and the island are as familiar as a street in which I have lived. It has been silhouetted against sunset for much of my life. From the mainland on clear nights you can glimpse its lighthouse, glimmers that stood between me and the whole dark – beyond, the Indian Ocean takes off for Africa. So it was a place to long for and from, the place on which I first concentrated such feelings as longing, a to-and-fro place against which to map all my comings and goings since. And as good a place as any in which to have had our honeymoon, beginning this true-love story with a so-far-so-good ending and no fear of angst.

Angst is unpopular these days, but I agree with those – from Rainer Maria Rilke to Leonard Cohen to Nick Cave – who tell us it is instructive. Making the best of things is a hard-won skill and I strive hard for it, but I also insist on my right to angst, and for countless reasons, all ordinary and domesticated and historically specific. Not least of which was new-age wisdom pouring from the airwaves then about there being no rehearsals for life, about how it consists of time spent while your eye is trained on the future, advice Ross and I were taking to heart while we were still so oblivious to the fact of being alive that we took it for granted.

We know better now, of course, having explored more of this planet on which we tumble about than the bits on which we grew up, and now we are closer to being 'rolled round in earth's diurnal course' ourselves. We know for certain, for example, that it is just as true that while you are making plans, death also happens.

Being kissed by a boy in the sandhills I am all future, set to go off. Instead, alarms do it, saving my virtue. Rottnest is in the grip of great storm. Lightning tears across the sky, thunder swallows the island and the Bathurst Lighthouse is like the finger of god every time the sky lights up.

The pretty-faced boy and I race back to the settlement and join in the effort of tying up boats, although there is little anyone can do but watch. The sea foams around the jetty. Boats wrench themselves away from moorings. We shout into the wind and rain, such drama being nothing less than we expect of life.

When I enclose myself in lattice on a cottage verandah this time, it is to read *The French Lieutenant's Woman*, and I know exactly which ending I choose. The man I will marry is about to take root in my life as substantially as the Moreton Bay figs flanking the settlement road. He will be no pretty-faced boy – whose name I have quite forgotten – but with him I am soon to discover the difference between being kissed and kissing.

Of course, I have no idea of what is coming when I catch the ferry home one hot afternoon that summer. I have learned to traipse down to the Rottnest jetty. Cool. Cool. Men have walked on the Sea of Tranquillity; it would not do to appear excited about *The Islander*. I am going back to a family whose destiny is about to alter. My mother has turned out to be right about death; it is only a matter of time. Loss will confound us all and in the wake of it I will leave home for good.

Years later, and I am at Rottnest again, sifting the dark for blessings. Ross and I have always preferred off-seasons and have opted for the far end of Geordie again, thrilled to have got it.

It has become astonishing to think we spent our honeymoon three cottages away. We watched sunset from the end of the jetty, eating chocolate-coated mint ice-creams, watching stocky cod tailing in the bay, faces down in kelp, their tail fins breaking the surface and inscribing circles on the air. At first we thought it must be a mating ritual, but at the restaurant where we ate dinner by candle- and firelight, a waiter explained in an unexpected French accent, *zat zey also* were only feeding. Ross and I ate meticulously after that, reducing each other to tears of laughter.

We are as reclusive this time as we were then, but this time because it is so long since we spent a string of days and nights alone together. Our silences have acquired ruffles. We make small efforts to please each other, as subtle as the gull shadows passing across the beach.

Journal fragment, Rottnest

Kate and Nan are young women now; of course they want to leave home. Nan's turn, time for me to let my youngest child go. No, that way misery. First, a few days of solitude. Together. My love and I. Their father. Their mother. Practising to be a couple again. Watershed…

It goes well. Over the next few days Ross and I reassure each other, are turning out to be good at it, despite nervous air between us. I keep having ideas. 'Let's take photographs, sketch, read, make it a fruitful time.'

He keeps wanting to leave. 'Let's go, get out into the wind, blow cobwebs away.' Distraction tactics.

One day we cycle twenty kilometres, climb rocks, walk beaches, reclaiming the island. On the other side Ross climbs into the hull of a rusting prow jammed against wave-bashed rocks and warnings are wrenched from me. You look out to sea here and the next stop is Antarctica. I see how afraid I am of his death and in that moment know I truly want to be the first to go. Then I feel selfish. Then I feel foolish for feeling selfish.

We spend an afternoon at West End collecting glass fragments that wash over and over themselves among the shells there: a glass harvest, sea lozenges. I place them on the bedside table in a plastic sugar bowl, where they promise to become smalti for a surface I can't yet imagine.

It is late when we ride back along the deserted road. A break in the weather is a window out of winter. Moonlight pours across the dunes like cream and the sea just waits there.

'God,' Ross says, 'this is magic. The wind puts you back in your skin.'

Back at the cottage we sit by the fire, inventing scenarios about how life will be from now on. Being alone together, the stuff of special occasion for as long as we can remember, is about to become the daily texture of our lives and we are still discovering it does not come altogether naturally.

Journal fragment, Rottnest

Ross and I made love in front of the fire tonight.
There's something about the way people long married
can make love, intricate and knowing, something utterly
perfect. Ravel's Adagio sprinkled its mix of melancholy
and jubilation over us afterwards, until rain started
beating on the roof and wind blew up off the sea with
such incredible ferocity we had to shout at each other to
be heard. I remember another storm here, years ago...

It strikes me now that there is something about dropping love into the heart of a paragraph like that – the heart of the matter, the thing that counts, a sentence that floats on a lifetime. Later, with the wind still forcing its way under the windows, I knew Ross would be keeping the bed warm. Without even waking, he held my hand and wrapped my fingers soothingly in his.

Three

A mosaic is a coherent pattern or image in which each component element is built up from small regular or irregular pieces – Peter Fischer

Last time I was leaving home to live here, the very words Canada, Alberta, Calgary were doors receding into my imagination. I would open new scenes at will, visions in which I never pinched my fingers with tile cutters, tore my hands apart on broken porcelain, felt confused, wasted, unhinged, misplaced. I had not the faintest idea what I was about to take on, was away on pumpkin pie and dormer windows and jack-o'-lanterns with misplaced hints of Salem and Woody Allen.

My enthusiasm encouraged Ross. 'We know Australia is more and more about international experience,' I remember saying. 'When we come back, our prospects will be better than if we stay and wait for all this economic down-turning to pass.' I had begun to use *we* as the spell for invisibility it would become. We accepted the job he had been offered.

There were many reasons for being poised to take that flight. Once we were in the northern hemisphere a host of wonders would be closer. We had been to India but not yet to Europe, a fact that people noted discreetly, like a scar they were trying not to notice, because for Australians that pilgrimage had a certain compulsion. Even now, people assume Europe is there, inside you, as if it were something you ate. It is certainly the undercurrent of any serious conversation about art, and my job title was mistress of art.

So I had begun to feel oppressed by living beneath the planet. I craved elsewhere, anywhere. The thought of being a traveller again seemed to enhance the world just because I would be on the move, or living not where I belong.

I remembered long, hot, dusty days in India containing far too many footsteps, but at the same time I seemed to be breathing through all my senses. Even in Delhi and Agra, when rain seemed destined never to arrive and I was leaking with loneliness, the very fact of being a stranger made me feel alive in a way I have not forgotten. Such memories had me filling with excitement while Ross was contemplating his new future on our front verandah.

That was at the very beginning of becoming this woman who will be better-equipped for the business of starting all over again, more able to revel in being an outsider for its own sake, who knows it is about to become her cover, a camouflage. There were odds and ends to be learned first, before my hard-earned talent for solitude would emerge.

Ambivalence is the pitfall: arriving in Canada last time, I also half-expected our lives to come apart at the seams. I could not yet foresee us living near snow-covered mountains where deer would be topiarising the hedge, or a day when I would stand looking at my Canadian garden and think it seemed extraordinary that *peony* could ever have been a word I associated with purely literary gardens. I was being transported into the world of glacier, mountain, prairie, ice and snow, deer, beaver, skunk, bear, woodpecker, hummingbird, all hitherto small strings of letters naming realities whose beauties I could not really visualise.

Canada was an abstraction. We had to discover for ourselves Aunt Jemima pancake mix and real maple syrup and cinemas smelling buttery with popcorn, long before that North American aroma invaded theatres at home. We had to see a beaver's lodge, moose tracks huge in the snow; had to walk on a solid lake, feel minus-thirty on our skin, its iron cold freezing our very eyes and reaching through our nostrils for our lungs; had to learn how dirty ice and snow become off the faces of postcards; had to watch for ourselves the seasonal stopping and starting of rivers and trees.

I remember first encounters with the phenomenon spring is here, the thrill of Canada geese flying down avenues in honking pairs, and their lime goslings huddled under the great draped wings. We marvelled through West Australian eyes at countryside lit annually by the 'green fuse' of poetry, at the sudden blossoming of summer to follow, a seasonal rhythm that fends off sameness, boredom, complacency. I had to walk among trembling aspen, poplar, fir forests on my own two feet, needed to stand on a mountain to understand how sublime its reach can be.

Of course, it was not all ravishment. Most Australian women are not used to being unsure of their feet, and it was to be my first experience of shoes having no traction in winter. The first time I fell I was mortified, more so when no one appeared to care. I learned to like shoes with soles akin to snow tyres – sorry, tires. Every time I picked up a bottle or jar it would be French side up. Every recipe I tried would require some ingredient or implement we had left behind, or would need to be baked for a different length of time because of altitude.

We had entered the land of the dusty diorama where the euphemism reigns. Women my own age seemed more conservative than my mother, most of them expecting to be addressed formally as 'Mrs this and that' by the children. They would be ruffled by words as innocent as *toilet* and *rubber* and go to their graves preferring *passed away* to *died*. My Australian crap-detectors were under full-time assault, so precious did this northern culture seem at times. *Nice* has real status here. It is worth reminding myself of this as I begin again.

My expectations proved to be way off the mark last time. At least this time I know the problem lies with the expecting. I was discovering that the truth of any impression lies somewhere between our powers of observation and our state of mind. I was learning that as an Australian none of this simply belongs to me. I was gaining my credentials as a stranger. This time I know a place has the power to transform you, and I am depending on it. This time I know a spectacular place is about to embrace us.

Flying into Vancouver then, its sparkling night geometry spread out below, I was bundled up in a window seat with Kate and Nan to watch our descent into that tapestry of light together. I wanted to swaddle them in it. Life had been transformed into light blazing behind a wildly perforated world. We were plunging into our future.

In which I arrived, passport in hand, containing its group photograph of Kate and Nan with me, their little faces all readiness; and tucked into it was the Canadian entry document over which I had hesitated but written 'teacher' in the box marked 'occupation', feeling a smudge of indecision in the spirit of new beginnings. I could only ever comfortably define myself as a teacher in answer to that query. It was the job for which I had been paid, a *real* job, until just a few weeks earlier. It would never have occurred to me then to wonder whether I should write 'wife', 'mother', 'housewife'.

In Calgary, the hotel stay that usually launches global moves is soon over. An afternoon has arrived when an agent is showing me through a house in Cascade Street, South East. It is close to Fish Creek Park, schools and South Centre Mall, which he insists on calling a natural attraction.

Contrasts with the old Fremantle house we have left behind are extravagant, but this home is a triumph of the lifestyle to which I am about to become accustomed. Such dwellings do not yet stretch by the kilometre up and down Perth's coastline; we are not yet familiar with walled suburbs announcing their presence by over-designed entrances and the manorial signs that signal a developer's grip. Perth's suburbs are only just lifting themselves out of 1960s salmon-brick oblivion, are still places you pass through on the way to somewhere, whereas Calgary's are already enclosures you pass between. The whole city is a conglomeration of suburbs crawling across grasslands towards the mountains, and I am about to live in one.

I am unexpectedly receptive to the newness of this house; its modernity makes me feel unburdened and contemporary and fresh. At the same time, it seems as if it could blow away in the prairie winds. Driving around Calgary in search of brick and stone, I have watched builders staple insulation paper onto timber frames that seemed merely flung together, press siding on in sheets, slip windows into slots, erecting jigsaw constructions in a process much too swift and insubstantial and effortless to my eye. Where I come from builders handle materials that strain their muscles, have ponderous construction schedules, labour hard and dirtily. I am used to the slow haul of cement-filled barrows up planks between careful stacks of bricks. So at first this house seems like a husk resting over its great cavity of basement, into which Kate and Nan refuse to descend alone until they get used to the fact of its existence below us.

It transpires, then, that in Canada there will be no verandah, no photogenic swing chair beside windows with shutters painted lollipop colours. It turns out Calgary is averse to colour in fact, and our Canada will be packaged up in a one-of-many brown house in a neat brown one-of-many development in a neat poplar-lined brown street two neat blocks from the girls' neat grey school. We have moved into a *communidy*, and it is not what we expected. But peonies froth along the back fence in spring, and in a small triangular garden beside the front step I grow begonias and poppies in spring and summer, colouring in the ground like everyone else in our street.

Seasons bring responsibilities, we discover. Neighbours are irritated if you do not rake your leaves in autumn, for example, so when Ross and I, enchanted by the phenomenon of autumn leaves, leave them there, our neighbours complain gently about our gold fathoms blowing back onto their lawns. It turns out clearing snow from the footpaths in front of your house in winter is also mandatory, as normal as calling them sidewalks.

So it might not be like the houses of my fantasies, but to us it seems cinematically vertical, with its upstairs bedrooms and dormer windows and angled ceilings. We have more space than we need for the first time in our lives, and the fact that not all of it has a pre-assigned function feels like being released from gravity. There are no old latches, no squeaking floorboards, no stuck windows, no aged linoleum, no blinds refusing to go all the way up. Curtains run smoothly on their tracks. Tiles gleam and are perfectly grouted. A house I can turn on and off at will, it hums like a living being, as heating breathes through vents in its floors and vacuum hoses run between its walls like a vascular system. Bathrooms and toilets, luxuriously plural, have extractor fans. The sink is fitted with something called a *garburettor* and an intercom connects kitchen and bedrooms. Everything works. There is not a hint of ghosts.

The garage doors open by remote control, letting me go from kitchen to supermarket and back without setting foot outside, a dedication to interiority of which I disapprove initially, but in my first prairie winter I discover how much more there is to snow than whiteness. This cold can crush you in a frozen fist.

Awe-inspiring temperatures also mean the house is triple-glazed. The sun can be shining in a porcelain blue sky and flooding the rooms at minus-thirty outside. It takes time for our West Australian psyches to adjust to this equivalence between bright beautiful days and plunging temperatures. At home cold weather comes grey and wet, temperatures make their way indoors. Being able to wear T-shirts and bare feet at minus-anything outside seems like a form of enchantment.

As do the chinooks blowing in to transform a luminous world of snow and ice to brown slush. I soon learn to interpret Calgary's sudden sodden ugliness through the relief these warm winds bring, learning to negotiate the muddy violence they do to clean shoes and clothes and spirits. Canada has turned out to be a place with a repertoire of shoes and clothes no uninitiated Australian could have anticipated. As for spirits, mine are becoming as changeable as that mountain wind.

Journal fragments, Calgary
How fabulous to be in a country with a border you can cross. Distances between us and the world are so altered that hitherto faint imaginings have become things we might actually do: spend the next school holidays rafting down the Colorado River, stand on the lip of the Grand Canyon, drive to New York, walk the streets of San Francisco, be somewhere near Salinas…I am swept away by a sense of proximity…

Our West Australian sensibilities are prodded constantly by phenomena as various as cowboy clothes, chowder, the romance of rivers with names like Kicking Horse and passes like the Road to the Sun, the narrow escapes of forgetting to drive on the other side of the road or to say the obligatory 'You're welcome' when thanked, let alone festivals like Thanksgiving, Stampede, Halloween, the minutiae of transplantation…

Alberta's soft summer arrives, our first. Alberta is a fine location from which to look back at Western Australia; they are places of similar largesse. If I ignore the mountains triangulating blues across the skyline, I can think myself back to the coastal heath around Cervantes, where space is also so abundant that cloud shadows mark the land. We go exploring.

This being ranch country, I am often reminded of the turn-off at home, gravel beneath tyres, cough of wheels crossing cattle grids. Versions of my mother's gardens surround prairie houses with the same wide verandahs, that welcoming front door open even before a car pulls in. The shapes of a farm are different, however: Canadians have barns, not sheds, rooflines are unfamiliar, hay is piled in the great spools that would come later at home but which at the time make me miss the block symmetry of my father's haystacks.

But stubble textures the light here too. Wild mustard and canola fill paddocks with yellows as exuberant as any we know when the everlastings are in bloom. When homesickness sets in, which it does like a deep ache, we take to the prairies. Fence lines reeling away over the rolling land are a perfect consolation, a kind of transition.

Kate and Nan can be bored on our long drives and retreat into their Walkmen, or Virginia Andrews' novels, or Paper–Rock–Scissors or I Spy, or they compete at spotting white horses and palominos, subsiding into whatever distraction they can muster. With them cocooned in the music of Michael Jackson and recycled Abba, Ross and I follow undulating grid roads and watch, side by side, what unravels, talking our way into a new balance, about home and everyone in it, what we are doing here, money and how to manage it, issues as unpredictable as the future and as immediate as furniture. With me not being allowed to work, this move has unforeseen costs, but these will be the girls' childhood memories, so a home we must make. We economise, dream, fantasise, plan. The world: through each other's eyes while we embrace a new pragmatism.

After a while these stretches of joy are meted out, though, and I begin to be weighed down by a sense of the planet hanging between me and anywhere I can feel normal. I have begun to have two lives. Blank weekdays line up between a string of weekends when Ross and the girls are home and we can go exploring: the prairies, the badlands, Banff, Lake Louise, Emerald Lake, any number of spectacular mountain places. Then Monday arrives and another week behaves as a long, undifferentiated day. There is plenty to keep my mind occupied, not least the drama of the Rocky Mountains serrating the skyline through our kitchen window, but eventually I begin losing my battles with a growing restlessness.

Journal fragments, Calgary
I saw a real cowboy today – Cuban-heeled boots, embroidered shirt, the white Stetson Calgarians are so proud of, an ostentatious, ornamented belt buckle at his waist. To me he looked like an actor between rehearsals,

or on his way to a costume party, but he was for real, a man in working clothes that just happen to be this far a cry from my father's dungarees and Martin's overalls and Ross's suits, just a man with different history.

History is sprinkled with words like *Indian* and *reservation* and *tribe*. The realities climb down from the Saturday-matinee screens of our childhoods. This is an actual place of cowboys and ranches and the peoples for whom their presence has changed everything. Calgary began as a fort in the homelands of the Blackfoot, Peigan, Sarcee, nations that preceded the cavalry and the prairie settlers. 'O Canada, our home on native land...' is a well-known local parody of the national anthem I'm told...

Stampede. The city revels. Ross's office holds a ritual Stampede breakfast for which we dress up in clothes from Lammle's, the girls and I fringed and leathered and full-skirted. Ross makes a convincing cowboy. The word *western* means something cultural as well as geographic here and it is unleashed for the parade.

Covered wagons, cowboys, ranchers, wranglers. Chiefs in full feathered regalia, magnificent, most of them old, ride their horses through the city. We find ourselves traipsing in a line of gawking, bored, diffident tourists through a tipi erected behind the Saddledome. Scowling black-haired women in their authentic fringed and beaded dresses see right through us, how gauche and easily impressed we are by the annual drama. They swap cynical smiles that no doubt have something to do with being turned into living artefacts...

Such unmediated encounters would soon be impossible to replicate, as graffiti began to complain from walls and sidewalks about the politics of the great rodeo. Its treatment of animals as well as people needed to change. Canada seemed to be doing better than Australia at shifting aside the still taken-for-granted colonial arrangements to make room for justice, but never well enough soon enough.

Friends wanted us to overlook this aspect of their history, liked us to see everything about Alberta as progressive and enlightened, especially themselves, when in fact they could be self-satisfied, complacent people. Right-mindedness was already twisting itself out of shape to become what would be dismissed as 'political correctness', that throwing out of babies with bath water. All this meant Ross and I did some growing up about Australia's national folly in those years. Seeing it through the lenses of unfamiliarity, distance, this prairie perspective, made our own country's dark history self-evident.

We were learning from our children, too. Nan's and Kate's social studies curricula concentrated on Canada's history and geography, so their homework was teaching us the wonders of buffalo jumps, badlands, sun dogs, the aurora borealis, grizzlies, wolves, log cabins, mounties. Nan, who would never become relaxed about the geography, social fabric and history of her own country even after we got home, learned to plait her hair in a tipi at Camp Chief Hector. Being older, Kate had a map of Australia pinned to her wall before our first year here was out, on which she had marked Cervantes and Fremantle with gold stars. But she is a proficient skater and skier and has an international soul because of her childhood here. We are all revised people because of those years.

As it happens we have left behind a controversy in Australia about converting cars to gas. Losing concentration, I say to a salesman expounding the virtues of a car he wants to sell us, 'Oh, it runs on gas!'

'Most of 'em do, lady,' he replies, flipping down the sun visor on the passenger side. 'Gotta mirror here, for the little lady, sir,' he says to Ross, assuming I am an idiot and making no further eye contact with me.

I have been reading biographies, finding my Canadian feet. Making an effort to be sociable at some office dinner or other, I enthuse about Prime Minister Trudeau. Western oil people inhale sharply around me.

'If you call it lucky to be robbed blind,' a voice declares.

'Ontario still sucks us dry,' says another, offering a sliver of explanation. 'This is Alberta. Mr Trudeau was never for us. They threw tomaydoes at Trudeau out west here.'

'He's seen as a shining example in Australia,' I generalise shoddily. 'For taking in the American conscientious objectors during the Vietnam War. Ours had nowhere to go.'

'Vietnam was no war. If it was a real war, we'd have been in it,' someone replies in a voice that bespeaks certainty about the national virtue. Images of napalm flash through my mind, and conscripted friends, and marches, and the waves of desperate boat people.

I am forgiven for my unwelcome opinions, however. I am a newcomer. I cannot be expected to get it right. With a pervasive impulse towards kindness, people assume they will set about teaching me everything they know, unconscious of their condescension. Parochial certainties are alerting me to our own, however, and what seems like startling provincialism soon gives way to recognition; in no time the persistent east-versus-west conversation has me feeling right at home.

Meanwhile, I am learning to use the sticky pleasantries of this culture not my own: sir, ma'am, have a nice day, you're welcome, washroom, bathroom, little girls' room… All trivial and entertaining curiosities at first, but they meet the usual fate of novelty. My part in social conversation increasingly becomes a silence I try to fake as interest. After a while I just cannot make myself happy in my new world.

I try. I get up at the same time as Ross and the girls and pack everyone off with lunches, brisk kisses, rides to school, but am becoming a careful performance of myself. Some days after walking the girls to school, or shopping for milk, bread, usual household necessities, I return to pace around in the large blue-carpeted silence of our house, increasingly preoccupied with inventories of loss. This time last year I had friends, students, so much work to do I could rarely get to bed before midnight. I ran community workshops and had more projects on the go than I can list – and I do find myself listing them, as if to recall that such energy was real. More and more I go back to bed and secretly sleep hours away, unable to imagine I could ever have been that other spinning, whizzing woman. Somewhere along the way, the move has begun to feel like a mistake.

I try harder. Homemaking is my cover. I push myself through the business of preparing meals, laundry, cleaning, because I never expected it to be all I would do. I develop an obsession with the cleanliness of walls and clean some wall or other every day. I begin turning on television to staunch afternoon silence and use ironing as an excuse for becoming addicted to *Donahue*, telling myself it is a cultural experience after all. By the time the girls come home from school I am listless and tired and often want them to occupy themselves and let me rest, and when they don't, I am bad-tempered and unreasonable. Their faces tell me they do not understand what is happening to their mother.

Lovemaking would require too much energy, too much dismantling of the mental scaffold I erect to get me through the day. Rejected, Ross's face can be as revealing as Kate's or Nan's. He blames himself for tensions between us and for too long I let him, persuading myself that he has a new job – complicated, rewarding, preoccupying – his mind will be on that while I do my vanishing.

Eventually Ross, Kate and Nan are a mirror in which I can no longer find the reflection I am used to. I sense the danger, feel the soul-crushing, know I must pull myself together. Making a huge effort, I set about joining the local library. It has become such an event to be leaving the house that I choose a suit from among my work clothes hanging mournfully in the wardrobe – closet.

I am overdressed for the library, feel inappropriate, stared at, intensely self-conscious, but I cling to my plan to read all the books I have never had time to read. The list is rampant: *War and Peace*, *Madame Bovary*, *The Executioner's Song*, *The Valley of the Dolls*; Walt Whitman and Emily Dickinson, and the rest of Henry James and Dickens. I make an assault on *Finnegan's Wake* and for a while am to be found walking around the house enunciating Joyce's mad text to my scrupulously clean walls, but I am too preoccupied to take much in, even reading aloud, which pundits tell me is the key. I am aware of my privilege in having leisure for this grand autodidactic effort, so I stick at it for several months, stolidly counting my blessings, but it never becomes satisfying. Not only because the list keeps growing and can never be achieved, but because it began on a false note. I am seeking ways to convince myself that being here could be a form of progress, but I lack conviction.

The idea of making my own art has dissipated. No matter how hard I look I cannot find inside this listless woman the woman who did those things – I am not the real thing, then, since everyone knows a real artist would be compelled by misery to create, surely the garrets and attics of history prove that. A *real* artist could never imagine coming to this surely: an accidental discovery of needlework which had never interested her before; taking up cross-stitch, being rescued by it, because she has had to sew badges onto her daughter's school jacket and during a quest at Woodward's for needles and thread has been seduced by the colours of embroidery cotton.

We still have the cushions I worked. At home I could turn and run my fingers over those frantic stitches to summon up that woman more lost in silence than I am now, that other beginning, a raw time when she was unskilled at this business of being submerged in anonymity, solitude, and encountering for the first time a sense of loss and self-doubt that is peculiar to being transplanted.

Among challenges to be faced in any new city are finding doctor, dentist and hairdresser. Eventually I work up the courage to go downtown to have my hair done, having discovered that something so ordinary can demand courage, but still determined to save myself.

Afterwards I leave the salon, looking like tumbleweed with legs but more distressed by the hairdresser's parting hostility. I am lost among plus-fifteens trying to find my way back to the LRT station when I realise I forgot to tip, a transaction I have yet to learn to remember. Anything less than a standard ten percent rattles even the determined courtesy of Canadian service, while my Australian consumer self still regards tipping as an extra cost of living. When, where, how much: these are skills I have not yet acquired, and having forgotten brings on frustration at my own incompetence.

An unexpected effect of this failure is that on the train I am suddenly all head and beating heart; my palms sweat. This time people really are staring at me, I am certain of it. Later I would have several such panic attacks, which would keep me more and more confined. When I do venture out, I feel scrutinised and judged, and begin seeing myself as I imagine others see me. At the same time, I am continually surprised by my own reactions, shying away from being this odd woman out, outsider, conspicuous unbelonger. At home, it is the very idea of *her* that brings blood rushing to my face and has my heart ballooning in my chest. A confusion of miseries is sneaking up on me.

Having started out using shipping cartons for a kitchen table and with the girls needing different seasonal clothes constantly, I have had no choice but to take the responsibility for shopping, but it becomes more and more of an ordeal. I am hypersensitive to supercilious shop assistants who say runners and sofa and living room and line-up, to my sneakers, couch, lounge room and queue; I say material, they say fabric; I say tin, they say can. This abrasion of vocabularies begins to strike me as everything from implied criticism to a linguistic duel, and behind what I interpret as a sickly commitment to serving the customer I think I sense contempt and find myself continually wanting to flee.

'I beg your pardon?' People ask over and over again when I speak.

'Your accent,' they say with a curvaceous *r* that seems intended to remind me I am not one of them, a self-evident fact in the face of which I have become pitifully and unnecessarily fragile.

Thoughts of real migrants, people who do not even speak the same language, only add shame to my misery, but there it is, I feel lost and battered by trivia. I falter, make mistakes writing my signature, stumble over my name. My voice becomes unpredictable, my tongue seems to be shrivelling; after a while my speech is ungainly to my own ear.

I spend too much time at the window watching women in my street. All their femininities seem movie-esque: they love big hair, their fashions are as different from mine as their English. I make a couple of tilts at reinventing myself, but reinvention rarely goes well. I homemake more and more assiduously, and the paint on our walls begins to wear thin with my wiping.

At the same time, everyone is neighbourly, absolutely everyone – insistently, demandingly neighbourly. Even the Welcome Wagon seems like a form of aggression.

One night at the movies I am afraid to stand in the queue when Ross asks me to keep our place. It feels physically impossible to step away from his side. Really seeing my distress for the first time, he is shocked.

'You're losing yourself, aren't you?' he says.

Trying to explain is like going to a doctor with a chronic ailment never apparent on the day of the appointment. If I know all this is happening and can describe it, how bad can it be? I sound ridiculous to my own ears. So I play it down and Ross suggests getting out more, taking steps, which sounds straightforward enough and perfectly practical, except when I am alone the downward spiral winds tighter.

One afternoon in a local supermarket I see a notice inviting applications for employment. Fleetingly I think I will apply and save myself. After pages of questions, the form asks me to specify a position. But with only visitor status I am not allowed to work anyway. I am an alien. It is official. I have documents to prove it. Kate and Nan are here as Ross's children, I am here as their mother and his wife. If I were to leave him, I would be sent packing. If he were to leave me, I would be sent packing. I am here at my husband's official pleasure, making his pleasure less and less compelling. I was forewarned, but rather than being forearmed, I find myself in a struggle against this growing sense of wasting my life.

Self-destructively I scrawl 'manager' and leave.

It is as if your life is hollow and has acquired an echo. The thing is you learn to listen for it with a kind of satisfaction and eventually discover it can bring contentment. Sooner or later you find other women listening for it too and learn that the effort of self-reinvention is enough to have in common when you meet. Eventually you learn that never having imagined coming to this, whatever your particular this may be, has as much to do with the limits of your imagination as questions of success and failure. But I was much younger. The bad moments, both trivial and substantial, needed to gather momentum before I could arrive at anything like insight.

Looking back I see how literal, sharp-tongued and inflexible I was; I wince at the self-pity. But I see a frightened woman too, stranded for months on a raft of deep blue carpet, wandering through rooms scattered with an earlier generation of packing boxes. Now that I can look back and back, as if through a concertina of lenses, she is a fractured being living in a cubist painting. Folds open and close, times come and go, the timid woman in the brown and blue house is tucked away in just one.

In the lived reality, she *was* lost. Home had been consigned to the past, and the past was behaving like a house you are driving away from for the last time – you do not want to leave because in some of its rooms you have left the really big events: weddings, births, funerals. You never expected to be, but you find yourself looking back, petrified.

Then, just when I had begun to suspect I had permanently lost my capacity for joy, my mother announced she was coming for Christmas.

It turns out Canadians revel in Christmas. They make it gorgeous against their white winter landscape. Enthusiasm is not seen here as faintly embarrassing. It is becoming more and more apparent to me that irony dominates most cultural activity in Australia, which makes us a terse, reluctant people in some respects, although we don't see ourselves that way. With distance I am becoming sensitive to this diffidence of ours, this fear of earnestness.

It is Christmas Eve. I have decorated a modest tree, a potted Norfolk Island pine stumbled upon in a nursery's exotic plant collection, of all places. It reminded us of Cottesloe and Rottnest, and crushing its needles between my fingers I catch a scent of coastal winds. Our usual collection of ornaments is stored in a silo at Cervantes, which my mother says was a perverse decision, since I must have known we would be here for one Christmas at least. I have made several of those, of course.

Canada has exquisite decorations, however, and Kate and Nan have seen to it that we acquired a few. Our tree is knee-deep in a tumble of gifts, and while it may not be resplendent, our austere little pine, a backdrop of gently falling snow in the window is decoration enough: white on white on white; white roofs, white-skirted, white-tufted firs hiding strings of lights that make nightfall wondrous with colour, almost too glorious, a toy Christmas.

It occurs to me that snow has seemed somehow familiar from the beginning, as if my imagination had been ready for it. Christmas cards? Irish nuns? A memory of snow deep in the hypothalamus? Would that be where fond memories of snow stowed away among generations of emigrants, to be handed on in their genes?

The lights outlining houses have already begun staining the snow blue, pink, yellow, green, red. Kate and Nan are playing in the driveway in mitts, tuques and padded jackets, looking like a pair of bright marshmallows. The fact that they are tobogganing adds to my impression of having somehow summoned imaginary places and lives into our reality.

My mother has become alarmingly fragile since I saw her last, but her presence is the tonic I knew it would be. She has made the house seem less like a pupa-case, and with her encouragement I begin to feel revived. Life is still something I feel a bit behind, aware of, a kind of glamour, something observed through a screen of unreality – so I can find myself suspended at times, like this, stuck, waiting for the moment I am in to become more than a picture of what someone else seems to be doing – but together we have already begun to imagine inventing a life within the net of immigration laws that allows me to do so little.

Instead of Christmas carols, ELO is playing in the background, my songs of the moment, about the durability of dreams, with Jeff Lynne wondering and wondering about feeling like the only stranger in town and whether this is how life should be, a question I have no idea how to answer. Melancholy songs have always filled my reveries best, these particular ones taking the words right out of my mouth.

For us it is exotic to be serving up turkey and cranberry sauce, and pumpkin pie with whipping cream – that surreal Canadian use of the gerund – all such a far cry from the salads, hams and crayfish of our family's Christmas tables at home. On the countertop, however, is a splendid trifle made by my mother to make sure Kate and Nan have an Australian dish, her usual luscious concoction that makes me want to sink my face into it and suck. For a moment there is promise in every detail of our world.

Except the treasured visit is speeding past and we have had to bring my mother's flights forward. The doctor has advised her to go home.

'Best she flies while she's still got the strength is all,' he has said. 'Australia is a very long way.' Whatever can he mean, *still*?

Ross has arranged to take time off afterwards, and to distract ourselves from her fresh absence we had planned to drive to the coast, to Vancouver Island. I savour the prospect of reclaiming that sense of adventure while I watch my daughters playing in the snow. The changes in them are fascinating. I notice that they both say Santa now, unselfconsciously, like the kids at school; Father Christmas is being consigned to the past along with other details of our Australian language and culture.

My gift to my mother for Christmas is an exquisite watercolour of Glacier National Park, a reminder for her of having been there with us. All that is missing from the painting are the deer that scrutinised us through the car window, so close we were able to look into their enveloping brown eyes.

Each of my gifts is a red-, green-, or gold-wrapped confection at the foot of the tree, a creative process that released some old desires and ways of thinking from the dark keep in which I seemed to be holding them. Since my mother's arrival I have been rediscovering myself, my capacities for imagination, concentration, even generosity.

So the world in the window is like a perfect meringue while I muse about our family's affection-filled Christmas conspiracies, watch my daughters, listen to their shrieks when the toboggan gains speed down the icy drive, see them turn it sharply and skilfully just before it reaches the road. Eventually they spot me in the window and Nan starts, new curves and hollows in her speech.

'Watch, Mom. Watch me! Kate! Kate! My turn. Mom, watch!'

Nan is all speech. She never stops talking. Ross will cup his hand over her mouth, but she talks on into his playful muzzle, in her now perfect Canadian accent. I wave, nod, watch, think about the maternal gaze, how it sometimes seems that without its confirming power experience becomes slippery and vague, about how potent it is, even at my age.

When Ross gets home from work we will go to carol singing at the lake, then the girls will go skating with him while I stay warm by the fire-pit with my mother. After that we have been invited to join neighbours for eggnog.

Looking forward to a festive evening I decide for the first time since we arrived in Canada that I would not swap where I am right now for anything in the world, which is when I turn around to see my mother holding onto the banister as she makes her way down the stairs. It strikes me in that small moment that Nan has inherited my mother's eyes.

'I just don't think I can manage it tonight, love,' she says. 'I couldn't keep anything down, let alone something eggy.' She tries a smile. 'Anyway, I think the cold will do me no good at all. I'm sorry to be a wet blanket, Lili.'

Her expression is strained and her skin is iron grey, but even as I am aware of this I wish her to be well, wanting her to be herself, as if she could always be that. I am self-important with the pleasures I would share with her. If she could, she would be going out to be neighbourly for me. That she cannot is my first real clue. Clearly the doctor is right and she should get the flight home over and done with if she is coming down with something.

'Not to worry,' I say. 'Will you mind if we go anyway?'

'Of course not, dear. All I want to do is go to bed. I feel as though I could sleep forever.'

Singing carols by a frozen fairyland lake completes this Hallmark Christmas. 'Silent Night' belongs in this snow-muffled world in a way it can never do at home. Afterwards, we drive back through snow-covered streets onto which colour spills.

I have assumed this business of eggnog will be a family affair. Such misunderstandings happen. When we first came I needed to confirm that root beer is non-alcoholic. This time I am wrong in the reverse and it causes the same hilarity. Eggnog is neither good for you, nor is tonight's gathering intended for children. The girls come across the road with us only to find our hosts and two other couples from the street immersed in a card game for which they were clearly not expected.

I have not yet adjusted to meeting people in stockinged feet, but winter departures and arrivals are complicated by the doffing and donning of coats, scarves, gloves and shoes at front doors. For some occasions women carry inside shoes and put them on when they arrive, but tonight our hosts are the only ones shod. I feel awkward and underdressed as our neighbour Cliff says, 'This is my wife,' doing a climb-into-your-eyes, southern-gentleman *thang* at me. *Can she be used to it?* I wonder, shaking hands with a tiny woman who is all smile and boots.

'Ross, my husband,' I say.

'Ross. Lucky man,' says Cliff, gripping his hand. Ross and I refrain from swapping glances at such clumsy compliments. We will save this one for a pillow post-mortem.

'Colleen,' the tiny woman says with outstretched hand.

'You two play any Thirty-One?' Cliff asks.

'Sorry,' Ross says, looking at me. I shake my head.

Kindly they throw in the game with promises to teach us soon – it seems everyone plays Thirty-One, even on Christmas Eve. Kate and Nan make Christmas wishes and Ross takes them back across the road.

Just as well, I decide. *They will be company for their grandmother.* Everything about tonight is becoming not what I had in mind: the girls at home, my mother sick with only days left to her visit, and Ross and I non-starters among card-playing strangers.

But Colleen brings food back and forth to her guests, keeps eggnog flowing, tosses around a neon smile, filling the living room with sociability. Both in their element in this city of expatriates, she and Cliff clearly love hosting gatherings of people unhooked from families of origin, calling them orphan Christmases. It is an evening I spend learning it is possible to let go, to do old things in new ways.

'Don't get me wrong,' Cliff jokes into my thoughts at one stage. 'I would ask Colleen, but my wife just does not have front-of-house legs and someone has to be in the kitchen.' He says it with a hearty laugh. 'Much as I love yew, Colleen honey, some facts just must be faced.'

I have no idea what he is talking about, only that I do not want to be complicit. Colleen ups the register of her smile into a laugh to match his and makes for the kitchen. I follow the smell of nutmeg to find her pouring jugs of cream into a blender and offer to help.

While I refill glasses, I say, 'You know, my sister had boots exactly the same as yours.' This tiny fact has drawn me to Colleen all evening, and the words are out before I catch them.

'Really? Down Under?' she says. 'And I bought these in Montreal?'

'Exactly the same.'

'You're lucky to have a sister.'

I clarify the situation for her, and our connection begins with a few strokes of sketching in central facts of our lives. It flourishes, but I contrive to conduct it during the days as much as possible, to avoid Cliff's incurable flirting.

I am still not quick, nor good at handling harassment or bullying, and even now I will submit to opinions and people I dislike, to avoid offending, or because something is at stake, or silence seems the best response, or I just get it wrong – *esprit d'escalier*. But less now than then, and looking back I see I have men like Cliff to thank for making the virtues of feminism apparent to me.

More significantly, I made a friend that night in Colleen. In the following months, over countless cups of coffee, her company would give weekdays back a texture of possibility: of someone dropping in; walks along the ridge and down into Fish Creek Park; cross-country skiing in winter, afternoon swims at the lake in summer; long, messy conversations about books and over games of Scrabble, Chinese Checkers, Trivial Pursuit, as well as the Thirty-One she would insist on teaching me to play. We shared the suburban weekday silence, sustaining each other in all sorts of ways as time passed.

Until we left Canada, that is, and we all entered the inevitable drift, becoming for each other people we used to know.

I make a home, friends, am at the beginning of several years I will spend disentangling my ideas of life from what is behind me. The prairies steadily become a place of comfort, the world opens out, light undulates over crops, wind spins shades of green and gold across endless space. The sky is restored to its proper size. The mountains put my sense of self back in its place. My mother makes her comforting visit. I begin looking up, am able to see the beauty of the world again. Finally.

I flew home alone for her funeral. The late-night phone call came only days after she had left Canada. My father's voice: 'You'd better come home, it's your mother. Lilith, she's gone.'

The thing I had been refusing to imagine. The thing you cannot imagine.

It is one time when money might make a real difference, but we cannot afford flights to Australia for all four of us, and Ross needs to keep working – providing, breadwinning. Money we had saved for a trip to Vancouver Island that summer buys my ticket.

It is a lonely flight, but this event would be marked by loneliness, layers and layers of it. The loneliness of having put her on a plane in Calgary, of remembering our tight hug and the back of her hand against my cheek, how she said my name as if she had something to tell me, but I wouldn't let her. She was ill, and she knew how ill. Of this I am certain by the time I reach Perth.

There is the loneliness of one small coffin. Our suddenly tinier mother laid out in a blue floral dress in a chapel, who must be left on her own in that silent, shadowy place because my father, Martin and I, still subject to the humdrum biology of being alive, need to sleep. It is the last time I will ever touch her, and her hands are dry and cold.

There is the loneliness in my father's voice out in the yard murmuring to his dog, patting her, 'Down to the two of us now. Eh, Lolly girl? Nothing we can do about it either, nothing at all. And sheep still need shearing, no matter what, eh, old girl?'

It would never occur to him that anyone could be listening; he is used to these rooms being empty. But sleeping in my old room, the bed narrow and uncomfortable now, I hear him through the window. What fierce pain it is to hear your father's private grief. That night I forgive him every flaw and misdemeanour my ferocious girlhood judgements had ever held against him.

There is the accumulating loneliness of being in a family struck by events that press the mind at questions more fortunate people do not wonder about, like whether the loss of your mother might in any way be different from the sudden, simultaneous plucking away of a sister and brother. I find myself calibrating loss, feel stalked by death. We all feel it, the three of us who are left. The exhausting, depleting loneliness of irreversible loss is back.

Being back in Cervantes is to discover how well Western Australia runs without me. I feel like an unnecessary part come loose in an engine. In the new status quo, Martin takes care of the farm and of our father, who is smoking again but there is no sign of booze, fortunately. He seems almost tranquil, so stunned is he by the fact that she is gone.

And I feel torn at, but not in the way being at home usually tears, as if it would wrench me back into childhood. This time the house is filled with an unfamiliar privacy, a quiet different from any I remember there. It has become a place that no longer belongs to me, and being no longer at home in my parents' house makes me long for my own, but my own is elsewhere now, far away and not supposed to be called home at all. Now it begins to seem more like one.

Naturally, my father and Martin have placed me in charge of food. For their sakes, I agree, forcing myself to think about cakes and sandwiches for the funeral gathering. My mother did all this last time, of course. It occurs to me that being the only woman left makes me feel trapped at the bottom of an empty well.

Driving into Cervantes for fresh supplies and passing the turn-off to Lake Thetis, I miss Ross and the girls more intensely than I have ever missed anyone, more intensely even than I miss my mother, whose death is impossible to fathom. Suddenly I am all wife and mother. Then, on the beach, enveloped by the sight, sound and smell of the sea and wind, my mother's absolute absence becomes real for the first time, making me all daughter. I do my crying there and seem to be crying for a thousand reasons at once.

Time rushes towards the moment when I am about to fly back to Canada. My father is handing me a rug I brought from Agra for my mother years earlier. Slipping the tidy roll of it onto the seat of the car, he says, 'She'd want you to have it, love. And here, you should take this, too.'

There has been no time for framing the watercolour we gave her, so incredibly recently. I see her opening it on Christmas morning and brushing her hand over it. She said, 'What a wonderful day it was. Especially the deer. I'll never forget it, my darlings.' a memory of her voice so vivid it is impossible to believe she can really be gone.

Wanting the girls to appreciate art, I used the painting to show them how the artist has predicted light and shade so well that no white paint was used and the paper is simply left untouched in the right places. We clustered around my mother, collectively impressed by paper-white spaces where what has not been painted is the point and gives shape to the rest. My mother was sitting beside me in her flesh and blood, where she will never be again.

'In light, white is the sum of all colours,' Ross was explaining.

So I stare at the painting and missing them all erupts into an overwhelming desire to touch her, them, in which death and apartness blur. Loss is loss. The time has come. The time has come to grow up. I must go home. And now that is not here.

I kiss the cheek my father uncharacteristically offers. Martin, who says he can't stand sentiment, but has suggested for the umpteenth time that he ought to be the one to take me to the airport, drives away quickly. I look back at the old house and the blaze of gravel dust behind a speeding car seems absolutely fundamental.

Journal fragment, Calgary

There are things to be grateful for, especially that she visited us here. Kate and Nan will remember her. She saw snow for the first time with them. It was like a gift they'd given her personally. She revelled in it, so we have these photos of her making snowballs and shrieking with laughter while the girls tossed snow around, pictures of my mother's grand-maternal joy. She and I watched freezing rain sculpt trees and marvelled together at the ice-lace that forms on lakes. We were arm-in-arm...

Now, reading this, other moments come back. How the five of us skirted a frozen lake, with the sun glittering on the great prairies of snow. How she touched a frozen waterfall and knew it for the exquisite oxymoron it is, stood gazing up at it, watched climbers whose lives depended on icepicks and pitons.

'If I was young I'd definitely want to climb one; it'd be like climbing an idea,' she said.

Nan, little then, about eight or nine, laughed. 'You can't climb ideas, Gran. They're not like waterfalls or something.'

I try to remember it clearly, my mother's delight, but it has moved further away. I know memories can be tuned to play what you want to hear; long-distance realities can be reinvented. Back in Canada, I was able to think of home almost as if my mother were still there. The gulf that her death was could be made to blend with the multitude of smaller absences built into living so far away.

On the skyline the Rocky Mountains went on catching the light like great swags of crumpled silk, steadily infusing me with a sense of inhabiting a planet. Despite everything, my imagination was being forced to expand, to accommodate independence. By the time I really began thinking of Cervantes as a motherless place, a sign of my recovering courage, Ross and I were planning our future with a new sense of autonomy.

Journal fragment, Calgary

The Icefields Parkway must be one of the sublime drives on earth. The mountains keep putting my sense of self into a new perspective. They hint at the grandeur of a planet time has already worn away on our southern continent, giving me a better idea of Australia's spacious age. Awesome conglomerations of peaks, they beckon and threaten simultaneously, beauty like an unreliable promise. At times I feel as if I want to be up there wandering among them until I was extinguished, drawn to the edge of everything.

Being raised to a sense of hospitable land shading off into wilderness – *its beauty and its terror* – we grew up with the same paradox, but the landscape we are used to pulls disappearing tricks. No West Australian imagination can be prepared for these extraordinary appearing ones. The horizontal become vertical, the out-of-bounds made visible...

We enter a ripening time. Ross and I are becoming really married in the big, comfortable Cascade Street house. Because this house stays warmer we are more often naked together out of bed than we were at home, the practicalities of sensual delight being what they are. We shower together more often, because we have a bathroom big enough to invite comfortable sharing.

It has taken me too long to give in to the pleasures of the bedroom, especially this one that seems outrageous with mirrors when we make love. Along the way I have become a bit of a prude; indeed, nuns are in my head like homunculi, but Ross is driving them out about now, has begun finding his way through the pores of my skin, coaxing a more sensual woman out of me than I knew I could be. In the comfort of this big Canadian house, we are getting used to each other, which is turning out to be anything but the marital affliction we were taught to fear. Indeed, getting used to each other is making our marriage grow, become; it has begun to seem indestructible.

So, when we least expect it, life blows us away with its capacity for being re-infused with wonder and potential. Nothing could have been further from our minds, but I am pregnant again.

Winter comes early, and for a third of this particular year the place is snow-covered. While Ross is at work and the girls are at school I rug up to shovel snow from paths and driveway, in a spirit of keeping fit. We have not lived in Calgary for long enough for this to be a chore yet, although Colleen assures me that if you grow up shovelling and being confined by snow and slipping in it and ruining your shoes in it, it loses its charm.

I remain firmly seduced. The beauty of sunlight on snow and ice, that spectacular relationship of melting warmth and sparkling light, props up fresh determination to find contentment on this detour my life has taken. I have spent too much time looking for ways to start again. Well, ways have arrived.

Alberta winters are bright and blue, so I sit reading in a sun-filled window for hours some days, waiting for my unexpected baby. Or I sit watching snow fall and daydreaming into its transforming power, the way it turns rubbish into piles of light, does away with straight lines. I have never lived in so curvaceous a world.

An early spring follows. Being more and more my mother's daughter, I have taken to gardening. Unlike her, though, I even find mowing a lawn thoroughly rewarding – done well, it's a way of texturing light – where she saw it as a man's job. Habits of mind about who does what are being vigorously contested, and in the spirit of the times I have decided on behalf of my daughters that I must resist the gendering of work, among other things, so I am regularly to be found guiding the mower back and forth. It seems little enough.

It turns out my forays into the garden are observed by a woman who has moved in next door. Marta will later confess to watching me do what she calls 'man-work'. We first meet on an afternoon when, obviously pregnant, I am mowing while Ross is on the deck preparing our application for landed residency. She comes over to introduce herself, believing her presence will mortify him, we learn later.

'I have seen your *Crocodile Dundee*,' she tells us.

Ross would try to convince Marta that such films do not represent Australian masculinity, but I am never sure she believes the man-work is my choice. Nevertheless, we become friends over these conversations and I introduce her to Colleen. Friendship enriches the weekdays. Our footsteps ought to be etched into the sidewalk connecting those three houses.

So Canada, spinning all sorts of unexpected strands into our future, has turned out to be offering changes of heart as well as scenery and lifestyle. When the agent writes to inform us of a shattered stained glass window in the front door of our Fremantle house – among other things, such as a dead lawn, water damage in the bathroom – we decide to repair and sell.

The decision is easier than we expected. Ross is surprised by my willingness to consign that home to memory after our renovating efforts there, but the comfort and efficiency of Cascade Street have turned the prospect of wrestling with the past again into a tiring one. Experience is opening me up to possibilities of moving on, living more acutely in my own day and age. I am learning to appreciate the new.

It has become normal to be coming back to Cascade Street, Calgary, Alberta. The address has planted itself more and more firmly at the centre of our explorations, and the landscape has been imprinting itself on us as we claimed Banff, Jasper, the Drumheller Badlands, hiking up to the bed of glaciers at Lake Louise, walking on the great Athabasca icefield, exploring the mountain parks. By now we have spent many a weekend camping – Paddy's Flats, Two Jack Lake, driving south to Montana. We plan a journey through

Arizona to the Grand Canyon soon, intending to go further and further afield when this baby is old enough.

Our only restlessness is a longing for coastal places. But once again a trip to Vancouver has to be delayed, this time for the joyful reason of a birth.

Journal fragments, Calgary

Canadians like their nests cosy. Their homes are more fabric-lined and titivated with occasional chairs, end tables, lamps, silk trees, flowers, figurines, flounces and frou-frou than anything I'm used to or can imagine ever liking. My theory is it's related to climate. We're a more alfresco people. Canadian lives have to be lived so much inside that theirs has become a padded, fur-lined, frilled and bundled-up aesthetic…

I've never encountered shoppers as demanding and meticulous as Canadian women, or men so involved in the acquisition of appliances and furnishings. Indeed, acquisition *and* furnishings. Our Australian culture seems scrappy and make-do in comparison; we are improvisers. I guess because the wardrobe for four seasons is complicated – an Australian doesn't grow up needing toques, mitts, scarves, jackets for winter, spring and summer, thermal underwear, snow boots. It's as if necessity and training make Canadians fastidious consumers, and the national psyche seems a little fussy and careful in comparison with ours. Such extreme cold can make self-care a matter of life and death, and I see how it would be the source of so much people-pleasing. Snow and ice force you to be patient, to go slowly and carefully. Perhaps all this is the source of the stolidity around me…

At the library café one day a woman ahead of me in a queue asks to taste the soup of the day before ordering it.

'How else can you know whether you even like mushroom and vegetable soup, right?' she says, flashing perfect teeth at the young man behind the counter.

He spoons a portion into a cup and we all hang on her verdict. I try to imagine an Australian waiter. 'Take it or leave it, lady, people are waiting.' But here, everyone stands patiently while she decides against the soup.

'Just as well you tasted it then,' the server says, meaning it.

No one else seems to object to standing for so long while a woman tastes one-dollar soup before taking the risk of investing. In fact, Canadians don't seem to mind a great deal Australians would never stand for, and are particular about a lot Australians are simply expected not to notice. The difference is clear in my impatience with this woman's charming certainty that her personal tastes ought to be so indulged. As it happens, I am furious. Standing for any length of time soon has me feeling like an imminent explosion, or collapse – battleship in full sail, yes, but it was never like this with the two girls. I put my irritation down to the awful pressure in my abdomen.

Later that week the doctor tells me it is only to be expected at my age. He is always on about my age. He insists I should expect a pregnancy to feel vastly different from how it was with Kate and Nan.

I was learning from differences in our two consumer cultures. I was beginning to be less laissez-faire and offhand about spending Ross's hard-earned money, having begun to think of it that way. The time would come when it seemed routine to make the effort of returning damaged goods, and of asking for what I really wanted in restaurants, even occasionally for something not on the menu, as with skim milk, soya milk, wholemeal bread, even after we got back to Australia. Back then the service in many an Australian café could be grim, even worse once you left the metropolitan area.

'Canadians are such happy workers,' I remember my mother remarking. And, 'Aren't they a kind people? Nicer than us in a lot of ways.'

So it was not just me, and none of it always, but these social and cultural observations trailed through our conversations like wisps of smoke while we were living here last time. We were encountering perspectives, theirs and ours, changing and being changed.

A particular difference, I was about to learn, is that when you are in trouble Canadians will risk intruding. In Australia misery is likely to heighten people's reserve and we are likely to assume others prefer to suffer in privacy unless they ask for help. Then we do everything we can. Voluntary kindness can be a form of courage, however, and Canadian determination to be neighbourly was to be my saving grace.

Even now I have an occasional dream in which the feeling of being pregnant lingers after I wake up, as deeply real as if my body had gone on remembering of its own accord, as if a biological memory resides in the body's core. Each time the experience revisits me I cherish it in a way I never could as a busy young teacher living through it with Kate and Nan, and then, the last time, here.

Although that was closest to the dream-feeling, perhaps because I was older and taking less about life for granted, or had the time to concentrate on being pregnant, or because my baby was so unexpected. That all this time after my ovaries have retired from their ineffable rhythmic delivery, my dreams can still reclaim the physicality, the utter corporeality of being pregnant, is like a delicious aftertaste of bliss. Bliss, however, was not always the feeling to arrive with dreams.

In this one I have fallen into a well and landed on a ledge from which I cannot quite reach the clammy brick rim. My pregnant belly is pressed against the curved wall, and when I look down I see a faint light far below me that I know is a tunnel.

I shout for help, my voice echoing. I can think only of the baby. Eventually an officious man pokes his face over the wall.

'I must not fall,' I call out anxiously, 'I'm pregnant.'

'Then we shall not let you fall,' he says, intending me to understand that the baby is saving my life because otherwise there would be no question of rescue.

He leans in and grabs me with both hands, pulling me out quite comfortably. I ask where the well ends up, as if we are merely chatting about the weather.

'Ah,' he tells me, 'that one goes to the seventeenth century.'

Dismissing me, he returns to what he had been doing which, as it turns out, was presiding over a vast formal dinner for fathers and sons. It seems to be a ritual meal at which boys eat at long tables while proud fathers watch from ranked seating along either side of an oval. While the headmaster rearranges himself in his academic gown at high table everyone maintains a disciplined silence. Suddenly there is singing, a war song, and the fathers join in.

Mothers are clustered in huddles and pairs along the drive or sit alone at the perimeter, just waiting, listening, fingering gravel, shifting their legs and managing skirts, trying to be comfortable.

I walk away from the well, my heart still thumping from having almost fallen to the seventeenth century, my hands resting on my belly. I am wearing a blue and white dress with voluminous sleeves that I loved when I was pregnant with Nan, only in the dream it is so long it pools around my feet, making walking difficult, or I have shrunk.

It seems this is an old and revered castle-school and I am here because I have applied for the headmaster's job.

'What you need is a headmistress,' I announce, thinking I could watch them eat, I could manage that much, but wondering absurdly about how ever I would cane them.

A passing monk reads my thoughts and answers crisply, 'Delegate!'

Suddenly, two young men are kissing passionately under a nearby tree.

'Don't you think that should be wiped out,' the monk asks?

'Not at all,' I reply, wanting to defend freedom, but the two boys look up and laugh derisively. It was a test and I have failed.

Dreams being what they are, I find myself standing in a garden bed cleaning windows and looking into a room filled with books and beautiful objects.

'I did not come here to clean,' I call out. 'You need an artist to take charge for a while.' But I keep cleaning, thinking it may be another test and I will prove myself by making these windows perfect.

Afterwards, on my way back down the drive past the banquet to look for Ross, I spot him walking up and down rows of boys searching desperately for a seat, but there is no place for him. Distracted by trying to get his attention, I almost fall into another well. This means the dream is going around in circles and I have not got the job – a fact I accept with equanimity, knowing I could never stand ramrod straight like the headmaster, nor could I delegate thrashings, since I reject the whole idea of them. I am desperate to work out how to tell Ross I have failed, however, that I will never be able to get him into this father-and-son banquet of his dreams, that he should stop searching.

Dreams *mean*. I recorded this one carefully in my journal the next day because it had alerted me to that prescience or intuition – call it what we will – that in unfathomable ways sometimes prepares us for what comes next.

Four

Each moment is not as fragile and fleeting as I once thought. Each moment is hard and lasting and so holds much I must mourn for – Jamaica Kincaid

Wisely, they hang a sign on my door: 'No Visitors.'

Had anyone but Ross and the girls come in those first days I cannot imagine how I might have behaved. Looking back, I envisage a poor Bertha Mason, am tempted to see a madwoman crouched on her bed ready to spring, could invent myself shrieking, growling, baring my teeth, but the truth is this grief had no such energy. It just emptied me out. I was limp, passive, crushed by great weight.

Two of us give birth to dead babies in the ward that night. You would think parallel loss would bring solidarity, but life is never so tidy. The first time we meet in the hospital corridor we barely nod, as if we are each other's proof of the unbearable new fact. We recognise each other in that looking away, that sheltering of private grief.

A desire for solitude grips me, but I summon up the energy and courage to speak to her. 'I'm so sorry,' I say.

A woman with wells in her eyes only wails unexpectedly, '*Mamma Mia.*'

I flee. We fall into a difference of language. '*Mamma Mia,*' come the cries from her room, without a trace of sentimental muck in them, only pain. I subside into the sounds of her weeping, as if she can do my mourning for me.

I don't know that I ever knew her name, only that I lay drifting in my own lack of permission to make noise and the syllables of her lament became part of a soundtrack running through these memories that still take up inordinate space inside me.

I was discovering why a family would hire mourners. Sometimes you cannot display grief sufficient to your loss. Its reality is pinned far down in you, it inflates, blows you up, invisibly. As if I longed to ululate, but didn't know it, didn't know how, we don't. Or to shriek, tear out my hair, wail, only in our culture we expect grief to be conducted in silence and privacy, and I am nothing if not compliant. For a while I could not bear to hear the sound of my own voice.

This was new ground. Until now true grief had belonged to the death of my mother. Somewhere deep inside me, because of her, and because of Dougal and Margaret, I expected to survive, had learned in a visceral way the truth of saying life goes on. The fact neither troubles nor dishonours the dead. But the prospect of surviving was what I most wanted to resist this time. I loathed the thought of recovering.

I need not have worried. It was a loss that would deplete me permanently. And it depleted Ross. It was the arrival of a silence we had no choice but to endure.

A bitter silence begins it. A couple of weeks before I am due, my obstetrician listens for a foetal heartbeat and hears a ghost. At the next visit, when his face tightens, I discover I have it right and something is wrong, and we have passed the time for patting me on the back and treating me like a child who inhabits, problematically, an old woman's body.

He leaves the room crisply. I hear voices, not words, just noises in the next room that eddy and form a whirlpool of sound by which I am intuitively frightened. Urgency has its own register.

When he comes back he instructs me to go to the hospital immediately, they will be expecting me – this is a clue. I am welcome to use the telephone to call Ross, not to worry, there is plenty of time – another clue. The receptionist has called a cab and he will be there himself directly – yet another clue.

I have become a body bag and must be emptied at once.

I am not litigious, or vengeful. I understand he did not mean it to happen. Still, I have finished with doctors and disclaimers, and because throughout my pregnancy this man has hidden under the cloak of old authority so that he would be unapproachable and unimpeachable, I will never go to a male doctor again.

My rage is also directed at god, in whom I long ago ceased to believe. I am aware of the irony as I wait in hospital, wondering what it means that yet again I am in the presence of death. My thoughts are predictable. I have failed. I have failed our son.

I wonder intensely about being the mother of a son, Ross's particular longing, this particular loss, because I know the fact that Kate and Nan are girls has never counted for nothing to me. Now we have had a boy, but he was born quite still, a blue baby, stillborn. Still born, yes, his birth transformed into an emergency that delivers this unforgettable silence.

I have been assured none of it would happen now. There have been developments in antenatal care, ultrasound. Less guesswork, more certainty. He would have had a chance, now. And certainly there could be no mistake about whether he was alive or dead in my womb. Things would be very different now.

Too late. That now is empty.

A doctor remarks, 'What rotten luck.' She might as well say, 'Shit happens!' I feel like tearing her eyes out, want to shout, 'Rotten medicine!', am discovering how ferociously the anger lingers.

People try to be consoling, reassuring, but one way of dealing with the pain of others is to diminish it, making it seem self-indulgent, a pitiful, insulting response. And the truth is, birth is never the safe experience they'd like us to think; babies do not always make it at all, not even with all our technological tricks, and not even now. Birth only seems ordinary because without it none of us would be here.

Some of us are not.

At first, lying in the hospital bed, I can think only of my baby. Even Ross and the girls flicker on the outer rim of a world I cannot see myself re-entering. Down in the small dark place to which I have shrunk, I have had time to think about how sometimes it goes the other way, and part of me would rather have been the one. I would forever be uncertain about my answer to the terrible question buried in that possibility of choice.

I am heavy with wonder about having given birth to a death. The brackets of existence have collapsed, although I know in ways no one else can that his life truly was a small tap tap tap at existence, when he stretched and his tiny hands and feet pattered across the other side of me.

The question slips out. 'What does it mean to be the mother of a dead baby, do you think?' I ask a nurse one day, thinking aloud. 'Motherhood being about life, it can't be meaningless when a birth turns into a death, everything in the one event. It lends a whole new meaning to contraction.' Pathetically, I start to laugh. They bring in a counsellor.

The older nurses begin taking matters into their own hands, dispensing personal wisdom while they take my temperature, check sutures, manage wounds.

'We lose the boys more easily,' says one. 'They seem less resilient, you know, more fragile.'

Another tells me confidentially, 'Sometimes they've just been here as often as they want. He was an old one, took one look at this place and decided he'd done it all before,' she says, convinced of some great truth in her words.

'Perhaps he came from the seventeenth century,' I say.

'Certainly, darling, could have been any time with these old ones, and any number of times, too.' She is pleased that I appear to be cooperating with her vision, goes on consoling, soothing, reassuring me with a practised kindly voice that signals how often she has witnessed this grief. 'Perhaps he's a soul who's found nirvana now,' she says.

I know he never had a chance to take his look, but because of her gentle fantastic murmurs my thoughts begin to trail an idea, the string of letters I learned in India:

nirvana. It becomes a kind of solace, strikes me as silvery and fresh, suggests another kind of arrival, a place in which it is possible for a soul to breathe. I allow myself to imagine it, my son somewhere beyond everything, a soul breathing.

Kate and Nan had no idea such a thing could happen. Their little faces are frightened when they come to visit and they are clutching an orchid each, the same as Ross brought me when they were born – flowers the colour of bruises. He looks at me carefully over their heads, tentative, uncertain that bringing flowers at all, especially these ones, is the right thing to have done, but to have come empty-handed seemed unthinkable.

These are the only ones it would have been possible to bring, a gesture of equivalence. I understand him. We fall into each other's eyes.

'Careful,' Ross says, as the girls climb onto my bed. He thinks I am made of glass. His own grief must wait.

Their gazes lock onto mine. They remind me of deer: careful, suspicious, vulnerable, frightened, poised for flight.

'Sorry, Mom,' Kate says, and the four of us huddle together and cry.

What I recall most vividly about lying in that hospital bed are beige open-weave curtains and a picture on the wall of two long-necked birds courting. I spent hours gazing at it. Sometimes the image seemed to represent me and the woman crying in the next room. At other times, they made me think of Kate and Nan, wondering, consulting each other. Mostly they stood for Ross and me, the way their heads were raised to each other in a kind of supplication.

Plans have to be shed like feathers. Gifts need to be returned, donated. You step into a time of dispensing with the paraphernalia of a baby's imminent arrival, then trying to restore home and routine to some version of what they were. You do what has to be done. And over the next while at your house crying is unsurprising and there are great patches of quiet.

As I pull it in pieces from the past, I still wish this event more than any other could be an act of imagination rather than memory, but the loss simply was, is still intact. Ross and I are revisiting more than mere memories by this return.

Journal fragment, Calgary
For years I could not think of the loss as loss. Wherever I looked was not a space where you once were. That would have been loss. Instead, everywhere is space you would have been, could have been, should have been. I am still sorry...

Marta, who has forgiven Ross for the fact that I enjoy mowing lawns, but can't help suspecting I brought this on myself by inappropriate physical effort, brings a casserole with her sympathies. 'Ah, your house is so empty,' she exclaims once, with her usual directness.

She has no idea. It is a husk.

Colleen comes and goes, never inventing reasons. Between them they punctuate days I would otherwise have spent in bed. Sometimes life feels like one long night.

This neighbourly triangle sustains me while Ross is at work and the girls are at school. A Canadian, a Dutchwoman and an Australian: Colleen, whose confusing tolerance of her husband's infidelities is coming to an end; Marta, with her abrasive tongue and ladylike certainties; me, with my chronic sadness.

There was less freedom to claim your loss, your grief, your dead, even each other, and we were far from home with no family around to take charge of the intimate terrain. The time for significant ritual slipped into our dislocation as if the earth had swallowed.

I have read since about long-ago mothers covering their dead babies with honey, not for its sweetness, but for its preserving power, reminding me of how I blanked out attempts to make something beautiful or poetic of his death. I could not allow it to seem inevitable and there was no compensation to be had, on this point I was rigid.

His sisters wanted to place a mirror on his pillow, however, having heard a story at school that it helps a dead child to recognise himself at the resurrection, whatever that may mean. Placing that mirror was no consolation to me; it only reflected the loss, shafted it back into my heart, as if grief could be caught in an image of a tiny face, suspended in an infinite recession, strengthened a thousandfold while real-life flames consumed it. But there was something necessary for the girls in it. Of hope, Ross said. So we placed a mirror.

Of course there will be memories. Not this time of handfuls of soil and the sound of bees, as at Margaret and Dougal's funeral; nor of my shoes and stockings and the hem of a blue dress and a smell of sandwiches, as at my mother's. This time they gleam with stainless-steel edges and smell scrubbed and therapeutic and have in their background the routine percussion of hospitals: tea trolleys in corridors, doors opening and closing, distant mechanical announcements, metallic things dropped and retrieved, unfamiliar voices murmuring in unseen rooms. This time it is my own body, its fresh seam stained with iodine, which is the visible sign.

New friends are kind, sociable. 'Best to talk things through, Lilith, get things on an even footing,' someone says. I have no idea what she can possibly mean.

Another describes how her sister, when her child Passed Away, had found a doll-maker to make tiny clothes and construct a coffin, and what a beautiful gesture it was and how, like her sister, I should go through the whole process as if he had lived, and how she could give me the name of the very doll-maker. The word *doll* crashes through these condolences like a disaster and I discover some presumption is too great for anything but silence.

At close range, presumption is hard to resist, however, and kindness can be overwhelming. Much of this comes from the wives of Ross's colleagues doing right things, and even in my grief and from within my prickly Australian reserve I know they mean well, but I am too often in the presence of women advising me to do what I have done, telling me what I know. Or their condolences reek of sentiment and I spend a lot of time feeling more insulted than comforted.

Life becomes a tautology. 'You have to face reality, Lilith,' someone I barely know explains, and I have a vision of my baby, hear myself telling nurses I wanted to see him.

'I think I understand the reality perfectly,' I say. 'Believe me.' She hears the slap in my voice and has the grace to blush.

Possibly I had alibis because we were in Canada. I mistrusted the system more, despised my doctor too easily, blamed more effortlessly, persuaded myself it would have been different at home. At the same time I was glad to be in this place called *Away*. At home the well-wishing would have been more knowing, more insistent. My mother, who would have understood, was no longer there. And I had no sister. Losses had collided.

It seemed easiest to let people at home know by letter, saying as much or as little as I liked, keeping pain at arm's length while I mailed platitudes. At the same time, some conversations are like rain: you sense what is coming and run to beat it. An old friend having just heard the sad news calls from Perth to tell me, as gently as she can, that she hopes I named him.

'I'm sure it'll be better for you, Lilith,' she says. 'You have no idea.'

I know she has never had this experience and cannot imagine what she means, but I refrain from saying it is none of her business, or that this is not about me. She intends to console me and I am trying to believe intention is everything.

'I think I do have some idea, actually,' I tell her, and leave it at that.

I understand it to be a name he would have had, not, as my friend would like me to pretend, a name he has, in some supernatural, Hallmark version of our family.

'Thanks for calling, Marilyn,' I say, as one does.

Journal fragment, Calgary
His name is between us, Ross and me and his sisters,
a mantra. When we say it, we know where we are, a
word to tunnel us through time…

Another old friend commiserates: 'Amazing how unpredictable life can be, isn't it? All the trouble it caused you
being pregnant when you got married, and now you lose
this one.'

Suggesting, I can only deduce, how much more
convenient it would have been for me if this had happened
with Kate. She thinks she is being bracing and direct and
intimate, this friend, but has always been tactless and I am
deeply relieved to be in Canada, where her insensitivities
can touch me only by the paid minute.

Marta goes on bringing her gifts of food and rakes up
leaves in our garden as well as her own. I tell her it doesn't
matter about the bloody leaves, but she insists. A kind,
formal woman, she eventually gets me past the door, out
again, outside.

Colleen comes and goes regularly, not inventing
reasons, calling, 'Gidday, Australia,' with an extravagant
accent, at the side door and walking into the kitchen
without being asked. This would be impossible to bear
from anyone else, but she just makes coffee and sits doing
her wonderful needlework, making no obvious attempt
to comfort me. Colleen knows what is and isn't possible.
It's why I like her.

There is a measure of reciprocity, for which I am also perversely grateful. She is immersed in misery of her own. Cliff has left her for a girl from work, star bunny at his latest poker night, and retrenched at the same time when the company decided to pull out of Calgary. He would soon be disappearing with her from Colleen's life back into the States.

Colleen refuses to leave. 'Going back to Toronto would be like being cast in the same role forever,' she says. 'In my family they talk to me like when I was twenty, or ten, or three, or whenever they last saw me. You can never be yourself at home, you know? Not actually. The person you've become doesn't exist for them and they don't want to know about her anyway.'

'You know the worst thing?' she tells me one afternoon. 'Cliff used to hold my head under the bedcovers and pass wind, thought it was a great joke. It turned him on. To think that for all those years I put up with it. How is that possible?'

I have no answer.

Journal fragment, Calgary
Pass Away? Pass Wind? How will I ever belong in this land of the euphemism, but how can we ever leave, how ever can we leave, how can we…

For Kate and Nan, this brother has soon become a bundle of precious and complicated privacies. They cling to notions of heaven as his destination while I am wrapped up in the consoling wisp of an idea like a fading whisper about his silvery escape. Ross is saying little, looking after us all.

We plant a blue spruce in a garden we know in our hearts will not be ours for good, but what garden is? A tree will grow here and it seems like an enduring symbol. Ross digs a deep hole, spends hours sweating over the task, fills it with carefully chosen soil, fretting about what might happen to us all if the tree fails to thrive.

Before long I have been scraped out and plucked at and told to consider myself cured, learning only now that some silences are necessary, they keep you intact.

It is still a time when international telephone calls are so expensive they are planned ahead. Determined to keep in touch, we take turns talking to family back home, all too conscious of the clock to be able to think what to say half the time.

For my father, a farmer, the weather is an inexhaustible topic, and because of Canada's climate he finds the subject especially interesting. He and Ross can do twenty minutes on temperature alone. Martin does his best with me, but has inherited our father's reticence. When his girlfriend, Cherry, moves onto the farm, a change I cannot imagine at this distance, she becomes a jumper-lead in conversations between Cervantes and Calgary, and I am grateful to her. We get to know each other as those cautious, disembodied voices.

That Mother's Day my father calls. It is late, his time, so he is tired, as well as nervous about raising the subject with me and making a huge effort on behalf of my mother, doing what he thinks she would have done. He tells me he was worried about how I might be feeling on my first Mother's Day, after losing the baby and everything. I am tempted to snap as usual that I didn't lose him, I would never have *lost* him, but bite my tongue.

'You sound a bit more like your old self, I think,' my father says, hopefully.

Long silence.

'You do get used to it, you know, love. That's the hardest thing sometimes.'

Long silence.

'I know, Dad,' I say eventually, knowing. Leaving grief behind is fearfully like an act of abandonment. How I can bear to keep turning my back on people I have loved is a question I ask myself over and over again.

Another long silence, but silences between my father and me have always been an eloquent part of conversation.

'How's Ross doing?' he asks.

'Not great.'

'Put him on,' my father says. They spend five minutes on the wind chill factor, both knowing what is really being said and comforted by speaking in code.

That afternoon I find Ross sitting in the lounge room staring out the window, looking lost. My first thought is that he is ill. He lets me test his forehead with the back of my hand, but is unyielding when I put my arms around him and preoccupied in a way I cannot penetrate. He has been reading Chekhov and in an accident of life has just encountered his own on a page. He hands over the book, open at a story called, 'Heartache': 'His grief is immense, boundless. If his heart were to burst and his grief to pour out, it seems that it would flood the whole world; and yet no one sees it. It has found a place for itself in such an insignificant shell that no one can see it in broad daylight.'

Ross's grief floats towards me on Chekhov's words. I have been taking too much, and for too long, and even now Ross doesn't want me hurt any more, so he doesn't want me to see him like this.

'It's just, I held him, you know,' he says finally, hardly able to breathe, so strenuous is his effort to contain himself.

An image slips into my mind from the hospital, when I had dropped my nightgown from my shoulders in front of a mirror and stood staring at my breasts, sore and so irrelevant I was filled with a sense of my body's uselessness, a kind of dread. I felt I had been wounded at the core with a scar that would be invisible, wanted to tear at my skin until I reached the site, wanted to staunch my grief but at the same time for it never to stop; it was a spring inside me, the source of being always mindful of this child of mine, who had been taken from me.

Mine, mine, mine, I think now, with Ross's book on my lap, the narcissism of my own grief striking me hard. He was not my child. He was ours. I have been hiding from Ross and he has been hiding from me. Something is sealed between us in that moment and I can't imagine anything Ross could ever do to make me not love him. I hold him in my arms for a long time – the rest of our lives so far, really.

All so mutually sustaining and nurturing, a fine reciprocal sensitivity between wife and husband, a relationship built on self-sacrifice, evidence of the love-ly little family – well, so it was. And also was not: we had been launched into a net of blame, too, all the self-recrimination and anger that catches at fresh grief and holds it in place.

There were days when I blamed myself, my body, a sense of failure consuming me, days when I'm sure Ross blamed himself, his body, for not being mine perhaps, for being unable to rescue me, us. Not to mention days when the girls didn't feel like it, whatever it happened to be, and took refuge in complaint, quarrels, their own determined misery. And there were days when I took it out on us all. How to describe the apathy, the despair...

A day comes then, when Lilith feels silence pressing against her, hard, has an acute sense of the prairie city's emptiness. Oh, Nan and Kate are in school only blocks away – that peculiar school of which she is suspicious, for its self-satisfied teachers, its strange fear of words like *rubber* and *toilet*, its purse-lipped principal. And Ross is in an office building somewhere – at the end of some long drive along freeways absurdly called trails, one giving way to another at high speeds so if she'd wanted to she couldn't find her way to him to save her life.

The city suddenly feels otherwise empty. No colleagues. No real friends. No family. No one she can call without reason. No landmarks. No old stamping grounds. No favourite places.

She is doing dishes when this tidal wave of empti-ness makes its presence felt. Thinks how she is always immersed in trivia when the break comes: the surge, this gut-wrenching rage, the ripping, tearing, rending and shredding of self-control. *The banal never goes away*, she thinks, *can never be risen above, not by me.*

This clattering of dishes is suddenly too much in the hollow hush of the house. Soapsuds breathe across the surface of the water, a rough and irritating sound. She plunges her hands into the sink, telling herself, *For fuck's sake, Lilith, just get on with it, do the goddamned dishes and let it be enough.*

Forgetting for an instant the scalding water.

She is thinking of use, usefulness, is bursting with frustration, failure, grief, talking to the walls in this quiet blue house, seeing endless uselessness ahead of her, sucking her into a vacuum. Sees she could be living in this suspended animation forever, that this could be it. Everything is an illusion suddenly, absolutely everything.

I am trying to wrap myself around nothing, by acts of will as small as twigs, bits, threads. A nest, then: I am this nest, and inside it, nothing, a hollow, a hole, dark, empty, nothingness. Every day, every part of me, an act of will, one small act upon the other, and out of the collection of acts is made a day, and out of a pile of days a Lilith seems to emerge. Only seems, but you would never know by looking that no one is actually here, that I'm a trick of the light, an effect of artifice, all the old habits of self-respect.

I have just eaten: cereal and fruit in the middle of the afternoon, a bowl of the hope that such substances will make me continue to exist, go on tricking the machinery within into working on and on.

I am doing these dishes obedient to a belief that small restorative cleansing acts will keep me going for another day. Task upon task, and all meaningless, through which I maintain this performance I have become. Order is everything, holds all the acts together. I am nothing if not conscientious about the holding of acts together.

A day begins with a shower, as simple an act as a shower. Standing under running water, I do sphincter muscle exercises according to therapeutic instruction, and exercises to restore my abdomen to whatever an abdomen is supposed to be. I perpetrate skin care, applying cream on cream to keep skin adhering to my body for yet another day in this high and dry place. I dress carefully, because who I am is who will begin to appear as I make choices: these jeans, that T-shirt, those earrings. I put her together with robotic care, intuitively choosing what to look like being the only act of imagination I will perform in a day. I do it for them. For him. And to keep the secret that underneath there is essentially no one, nobody, nothing. I have become a nutty projection of the nothingness on which you hang a self, the place where twigs, leaves, threads blown together might start hanging onto each other, behind which beginning there is only dusty space, some kind of grubby corner into which blowing debris would end up.

From which place I hear sadness in their voices whenever I rave, rage, rant, blame, sometimes pouring words onto the beginnings and ends of days like a thick paste of impatience. Words: tricks of the ear. Sometimes I throw them at ears and fling them into eyes like sand, am a sandstorm in a desert. And when it subsides? Nothing, except guilt and regret, regret and guilt. And sometimes words are impossible, cannot be mustered for any purpose, useful or otherwise.

Remove any twig that is this performance, pull on the thread I cling to and I, all of it, the whole composition that is supposed to be me, will unravel.

If I just close my eyes and wait, it will pass, she thinks, listening to the emptiness of the suburban afternoon. But instead, fear arrives, that this is a dangerous business now, not a game. This new act of will *is* a disappearing act, or could be, could so easily be...

So, *Just do the dishes, Lilith, just get on with it, for fuck's sake*, she commands herself, which is when she plunges her hands into the scalding water and physical pain becomes the last straw.

Screaming, she wrenches on the cold tap. Water rushes into itself as she pulls dishes from the sink willy-nilly, flings them against walls, onto the floor, back into the sink, so water splashes over her, the cupboards, the floor. Again, again, again, until she drops exhausted and leans against cupboards where she sits and cries, surrounded by bright yellow shards of broken china. Eventually, it stops. Crying always does, even when bleeding won't.

The only sound now is fizzing soapsuds, on the tiles this time, while her panic and rage subside and she begins to feel the burns and, worse, the cuts. Eventually, pulling herself to her feet and plunging her hands into the freezer, she accepts pain, which seems well deserved, and wonders whether blood freezes, decides of course it must. Then she wraps her hands in tea towels, anything will do.

I am exhausted. I will take myself to bed, just for an hour, to recover. Then I will clean up. No one needs to know I have smashed my way through a sinkful of plates. I am a decent woman, will clean up every trace. I will go to Zellers and replace every broken thing, except that will show up on our Visa bill, and he'll know. There must be a way. I will find an explanation while I rest. There must be a way to explain.

In bed she thinks her way down deep into hollows and nothingness, into thin air, past the nub, past all the small sad sounds the memories make in her throat, down past where the very idea of a self first unfolded and she bought the story of a life, down to the pith where there seems to be simply nothing, nought, zero, into the solace of sleep.

Waking up to thoughts of all that shattered cheap and cheerful china, chosen while we were thinking breezily of being here on a sojourn, an adventure, so choosing bright china by which we meant to be playful, having no need of serious household accoutrements in a temporary existence. We were setting up this home for just a couple of years – nothing needed to be permanent. So, yellow: a sunny reminder of Perth overlaid on prairie gold and the great canola crops beyond Calgary – we had this very conversation in Zellers, when even porcelain trivia could express our optimism about making a home here.

Waking up to shame, and thoughts of Ross, Kate and Nan, it occurs to me in flickers that I must be climbing back, since I am still here, hanging on for dear life to threads and insubstantialities that make up the thing I am, this self that is an effect of years of persuasion that it is somehow important I should be alive. Discover I am relieved to have made it this far back, to have managed my way to the surface again, am grateful somewhere for the meagre resumption of habits of mind that will mean this is how I begin, with the act of getting out of bed, this time with crockery on my mind.

Soon I have climbed far enough back that thoughts of nests have more to do with pink flesh around an accumulation of bones, how the threads are no longer dry and dead, but contain a beating heart, mine, and how the very idea that each day should be a series of twiggy acts by which I invent myself seems less terrible with the passing of these slow minutes. Compared with a few hours earlier the thing I am seems less a matter of shell-enclosed nothing and begins to take on a possibility of promise. At least there is a thought of eggs, yes, so fertility, bringing with it a notion of life, a sense of potentiality, fruitfulness, things for which to be grateful. I can sense a time when I will be glad of this resilience that means reaching wakefulness, finding a way to get up, clean up, when I become able again to imagine coping. Eventually I push myself through the great mental effort of moving, pull back the covers, force myself to my feet, to the bathroom, to the more careful wrapping of my torn skin.

In the mirror, the familiar blank lying gaze, the smile that says, *See this? See how well I manage the trick of being here, of seeming to be? And see how well I recover? See me, still here?*

She will strip the bed later. First, back in the kitchen, she faces sweeping the mess together to be disposed of in the alley bin. She slumps at this prospect, but rather than being overwhelmed, finds herself thinking how ordinary, how stunningly ordinary it is, to be squatting with damaged hands among bits of smashed kitchenware. To the part of her softly insisting, *You've gone too far, this time you really have gone too far,* she promises to gather up the pieces and use them, every last one, every trace, she resolves, every fragment, if it takes a lifetime. It is a vow to her better self.

Her injured hands make her clumsy, but with a determination that comes from shame, she gathers up the shards and stores them in a box in the basement. This time the kitchen is noisy with sounds of scraping and sweeping, her footsteps up and down the stairs. These are the sounds of ordinary housewifery. No one ever needs to know. You live in an intimate regime with a man you love and your two daughters, but not even they need to know everything there is to know about you. Not everything can be told.

She begins imagining what could be done, how you could compose surfaces that remind you of things you might want to be reminded of, and eventually something inside her begins giving way, giving in to certain facts, like that a person can make the effort of putting her shoulder to life and keeping it there after all, despite everything, instead of disappearing as she is too easily tempted to do.

Pique assiette, she thinks, remembering the old mosaic craft. Not for nothing is it called memory ware.

For a long time Ross would quiz me about that afternoon, never quite understanding how such wounds could be accidental. Stitches would run from index finger to wrist and my hand would never be the same.

'You sure are one lucky woman,' the doctor said, and I knew it to be true.

My story was that I had tried to rearrange the kitchen and the sideboard toppled onto me.

We were lucky in this: it was not a story that would divide there the way love stories often do, are so often made to do, the familiar stories indulging the impetus of a marriage going down, crashing and burning, the bifurcation of us, all the tales that would kill us off in the interests of a good plot. For their own reasons, they would have had us less enduring and resilient than we have been in the mesh of time being lived out together, which is the truth of the thing. Most stories would have wanted Ross and me disentangled here, and we came close to the possibilities they favour – the darker sides of us all flapped in the open sometimes – but we survived, overcame, rode out, located the day-to-day richness of life again.

Kate and Nan saved me. You have no choice but to get up in the mornings when you have children. You do put on the brave face of which the world speaks, and before long you fuse with this act of brave-facing. That careful visage oriented towards the world becomes you.

Minute by minute the ordinary has its way with you. I put on a load of washing and remove it from the machine at the end of a cycle. I iron Ross's shirts and the girls' school clothes, until one day I am ironing in front of *Donahue* and thinking ahead about what to prepare for dinner. Such effort takes on a different meaning after a time, becoming a sign of restoration as well as loss then slowly replacing it altogether.

A day comes when I answer phone and doorbell without regarding it as an intrusion and fending off the unwitting caller it happens to be. Ross makes pancakes again one Sunday morning. Eventually, we turn to each other and make love, each finding that the other really is still there.

We put one foot before the other. It is not, strictly speaking, a recovery. It is accommodation, adaptation, the steady development of scar tissue.

Seasons being what they are, a year passes and I find myself back at a window watching snowfall soften fences and rooflines, seeing it mould the street into curves, loving how it sculpts, feathers, hushes. Some days I am shored up by these delicate accumulations on trees, around the lake, down the slopes of Fish Creek Park where I have begun walking with Colleen again and sometimes Marta joins us. I watch snow slide under its own weight over the skirts of the robust little blue spruce in the garden to become a white crust glittering in the sun, until the next powdery mess falls to make that pure white untidiness that crystallises light.

This winter, snow is banked up along the drive where I go every day to pick up the mail, so I discover I still enjoy how it crunches underfoot. I am stronger physically, but this will be our first winter of hiring someone to shovel the paths and driveway. For some things I have lost heart.

Journal fragment, Calgary
Time sits absolutely still, as if it had congealed, curdled, frozen. Then goes by so quickly its speed takes me by surprise, like tripping over. The facts of my life have become not what they were. I am the daughter of a dead mother and the mother of a dead child. It has all happened so suddenly, like a kind of mutilation...

But snow, that straightforward enough phenomenon – water vapour frozen into ice crystals and falling in light white flakes – acts as a cool healing compress against my spirit. One morning the sun is shining in an Alberta blue sky and illuminating icicles growing from the roof outside our kitchen window, dripping spikes that appear to meet the distant mountain peaks in a glistening assortment of teeth, an illusion reminding me of perspective and bringing on runaway thoughts about things moving in and out of proportion.

Snow: how I will miss it, the glittering weight of it on forests rising up from the road and clinging in great wads to the mountains or falling in magical silence. Being drawn to the idea of plural lives now, in more ways than one, I could almost believe that in a past life I lived in a snowy, mountainous place: this country is so distractingly beautiful I wish Australia allowed dual citizenship.

Observing the icicles forming, as if by some strange process that was freezing tears, I begin to realise my capacity for joy has crept up on me while I have been putting one foot before the other and my heart has kept beating. For a while there I was pressed down into the dark, but there is something about life itself that insists. It is a stately force.

Five

For in that love which only has continuance, however
confident it is, there is still an anxiety, an anxiety
about the possibility of change – Søren Kierkegaard

Being an alien in Canada means every effort I make leads to some law of prevention or other. I would love to enrol in one of the women's studies courses springing up everywhere, so I consider going back to university. Hefty penalty fees make it a selfish solution. I make a stab at painting, promisingly for a while. Wanting to make a connection with some context beyond the house, I begin working towards a competition, only to discover I would be ineligible to claim a prize even if I succeeded. With each discovery that I have no right to participate at any level, frustration claims me again. For a while, not even the art for art's sake homily I deliver to myself daily can keep me from being disheartened. I am winding myself up in circles of ineligibility, coming up against my alien status wherever I turn.

'What competition?' Ross asks.

'Not the point,' I wail. 'And there needs to be one. It's about feeling relevant. It's about blind alleys. It's about what you thought you'd grown up to be. You have no idea.'

'Any success in this house belongs to both of us.' He argues this case incessantly, but I see concern in his eyes that even he thinks it might be less true now, not what we used to mean at home, when we felt we were working together, but each towards our own goals. Anyway, my preoccupation with connections between me and the world beyond our walls seems increasingly shallow and further proof that I am barking up wrong trees, impostor to the core.

And so it goes: short bouts of hopefulness, fended-off depression; self-management, boredom, distraction; until the break. Ross announces it coming through the door one evening.

'Women, we are about to make that trip down the middle and up the coast. We're off exploring. Don't argue, Lili, we're going to Vancouver Island finally, among other things.'

I am up to my wrists in meatloaf-makings when he adds, 'On the way, we have an interview in Seattle to become landed immigrants. You'll be able to do what you like.' He punches the air, elated. 'Finally!'

More vibrant air suddenly, with potential in its light again, and more substance to it in a split second than could ever be contained in this kitchen, oven, meatloaf pan. And from the girls, jubilation. Their delight is at the prospect of a holiday, but because of me they expect good things to come of being able to call ourselves immigrants.

Journal fragments, Arizona
Discovering that we Australians don't own the planet's heat may have punctured my sense of national identity. Over the last few days I've been hotter than at any time since we left home, but after

> a day of driving, desert motels offer swimming
> pool heaven. I dive straight in and the girls can't
> believe it of me…
>
> We pass Navajo jewellery stalls set up beside the road.
> So much turquoise and silver and gorgeous beading
> sold like flowers at home. It reminds me of India…

It may be true that the desire to gather up bright objects is a feminine characteristic. Certainly my magpie self is dying to stop and the girls keep asking, but Ross drives past, unwittingly exercising an unspoken power of veto by not taking us seriously. So much comes down to a sense of entitlement.

In an antique shop in Flagstaff, having been enticed away from our café lunch table and across the road by American history, Ross snaps when I mention that I have no money in my purse.

'For god's sake just ask me if you want something, Lilith. How can I know you want it if you don't ask?'

A scene I witnessed at the Fremantle Markets comes rushing back, one I would never have expected to be in. A woman fingering luminous strings of multicoloured beads said to the man beside her, 'Could I have one maybe?' A quiet, reasonable question, but full of longing and meaning: *May I, will you let me, is it possible, would you think they look well on me, let me decorate my body for you, my love, do we have the wherewithal, or if you have money with you, and since I don't, would you share with me?* But he only shouted about being sick of her tormenting him with her crap, isn't this lovely, isn't that nice, and no she couldn't bloody well have one, who made the money in the first place, did she, and no way was he wasting hard-earned dollars on this crud... He rants on into my memory in Flagstaff, foul-mouthed, mean.

She only replaced the beads and turned away, dawdling here and there, pretending to be a shopper with time on her hands, or a woman not quite sure who the man shouting at her could possibly be, a woman trying not to care, not to cry, accustomed to obedience and self-denial, but having wanted that small pleasure enough to risk asking. And it was small. I remember the beads, was compelled then to examine them. They were a dollar a strand.

So I turn on my heel in the Flagstaff shop, struck by the thought that Ross and I are caught up in a process bigger than both of us. At this moment it seems to involve the formal suffocation of wifely ambition and desire, not least for independence. Unless we are stay-at-home moms, as they continue to call us in the popular press here; unless, that is, the wives conform to the version of life that the world with its forked tongue keeps pretending has been consigned to the past.

A fully fledged dependent, I wait in the car – passenger seat, naturally. Eventually Ross emerges with the girls, all three trailing shopping bags. Unwitting, he flourishes a reproduced civil war poster at me.

'Can you imagine,' I ask, my voice shaky, 'ever pointing something like that out to me and asking me if you can buy it?'

'I didn't mean it like that,' he says, shocked by my fury. We are launched into the argument of our lives, the girls reduced to nervous face-pulling in the back seat.

'I didn't mean it like permission, for god's sake. Don't insult me, Lili. You know we've never dealt with each other that way.'

He is right, but it is not the point. Sometimes intention is not everything.

'Never have, does not mean never *will*. All I know is this. I have no money in my purse and no prospect of putting any there. You have money in your wallet all the time. Money in this day and age is what keeps body and soul together, and now I have to ask you for it. I have to *ask*.'

'You've never been denied a thing by me…'

'Denied? Listen to yourself! Christ, I'm an adult woman with no control over my situation any more. I want to go home. And I mean to Australia, where I can function. I've had enough.'

'Right, great timing! Just when we're about to fix it, you pull the plug.'

'You even pay for your own gifts now! I buy them on *your* Visa card. *You* get the bill! Look what happened at Christmas.'

'He says, 'I didn't mean any of this to happen this way, any more than you did.'

I am the one with the raised voice; I hear myself. But I see him see the problem. We will change our financial arrangements. We drive straight into Flagstaff looking for bank machines, which are new enough to the world that I still feel reluctant to use them, finding it easier to ignore the technological onslaught taking off beyond my doors and threatening to leave me behind.

Ross refuses simply to hand me a hundred dollars to place in my purse. 'Never again. It won't solve a thing,' he insists. We pretend to restore my dignity by having me take out cash myself.

That none of this is Ross's fault is the part I see, as he gets us through heavy afternoon traffic in yet another unfamiliar town. I see I have to find other, unexpected ways of being independent. The issue begins to dissolve in these confrontations and insights, just as we are on the verge of removing its cause.

Journal fragment, Arizona

These days everything ends up by some convolution or other on Ross's desk. I'm told this is an income stream I should learn to appreciate and manage, but someone is always damming ours upstream and I'm a fish out of water – perfect figure of disempowerment.

Well, yes, since I am in a desert as I write, and on the hills around us giant saguaros are holding up the sky with their picturesque arms, as if to remind me of what really matters...

Eventually we arrive at the Pacific. Ross and I taste it, roll up our jeans, taste it, splash each other's clothes, taste it. For West Australians, this is symbolic: facing west with an ocean lapping around your ankles is normal, it brings on fish-and-chip eating while the sun sinks into the sea. And in our daughters' delight at seeing us playful and silly we discover how long it has been.

Journal fragment, Seattle

Kate and Nan have become these prairie children who leave notes to a person called *Mom*. Our daughters don't

have our coastal consciousness. We've got them to the
coast in the nick of time...

In Seattle an inscrutable Canadian official cautions me
with practised affability. 'Mrs, um, Healy?' he says, peering
at our different surnames.

'My family name. A small bid for identity, you understand. I use Ms usually, or I did. At home, in Australia,
when I worked...'

'Ms is supposed to refer to women who've been divorced,
I thought.'

'Well, no actually. It was intended to operate like
Mr – you know, doesn't immediately announce marital
status.'

Smile. Silence. Smile.

'Divorce? Now, that *would* complicate things,' he says.

Smile. Silence. Smile.

'Hmm. Healy. Ms.' He uses the tone of someone
repeating the punch line of an old joke, and perhaps
he is.

Smile. Silence. Smile.

'Well, Mrs...um...Healy. I need to caution you that if
at any stage during this interview you indicate an intention
to enter the Canadian workforce, you will jeopardise
your husband's application for his family to remain in our
country. Is that clear?'

'Perfectly.'

Smile. Silence. Smile.

He decides pleasantly that he can see no real hurdles
ahead, we should hear in three to six months. He cautions
us not to make enquiries about our application.

'Don't call us, we'll call you?' Ross quips, but the response is humourless, implacable. 'No calls. You'll only delay the big day.' He doesn't share our sense of irony.

Smile. Smile. Silence.

Hence I am contemplating a new future while we pass among islands between Vancouver and Victoria, so many it is as if the gods had thrown handfuls of earth away here. This is coastline like cheesecake crust, a crumble of land linked by ferries with their bellies full of cars and cargo.

I sit in the lounge of one. Ross, Kate and Nan are on deck, but the wind is so cold I have come in for shelter and coffee.

Journal fragment, Vancouver
Gabriola Island. I try to imagine a life lived in such a place. Calgary seems bland from here, blank, dull. We're enchanted by these bitty islands. *Biddiness*: an American sound, a Canadian sound. Being here, we are rediscovering the sea, the sound of which right now I wish I could transcribe exactly, but it's hard not to be distracted...

Distraction just then comes in the form of an Irishman at the bar. A man used to filling a space, he is berating three young men wearing Roots Canada T-shirts about how sick he is of them colonising the cultures of the world.

'I think you're referring to America, and we're Canadians,' one of the boys says.

'Same ting,' their adversary declares, his brogue thick with aggression.

'Pretty rich, coming from an Englishman!'

Quick, sharp, perfect. No *esprit d'escalier* here, despite the soft-faced youth of its deliverer. A joke he has heard, perhaps. In any case the older man is too surprised and silly with drink to laugh. When I can't help myself he scowls in my direction. These young men turning away from him are like countless Canadians I have met by now: courteous, measured, never belligerent, at ease with their masculinity and solidly enclosed in a sense of identity. I would have wished for such confidence in our boy, had he lived to be their age.

They remind me of the men of my heart, my father and brother, too busy to ponder what it means to be a man, or what kind of men they are, without a trace of swagger, only an authentic ruggedness that comes from working the land. And no man could be more at ease with his masculinity than Ross. I like to imagine his poise would have been a foregone conclusion in his son.

Journal fragment, Vancouver
When Ross and I look back on all this we'll see
we've lived in small increments, this one made up
of islands streaming into the distance, our lives
reeling away too, as if before our very eyes. We are
becoming a concoction of places been to, time spent,
experience had, effort made – all past tense and
words that make me aware of our far selves heading
towards finality...

Turning that dark thought aside these many years later, I flick through notebooks with a sense that if I do it often enough there will be no order to what is remembered, just a pastiche of things seen, places visited. The North American continent is reduced to our slight encounters with its bits and pieces on pages that can take me from one extreme to another, beginnings to endings. Fanning through the various contemplations of my younger self I am grateful for evidence that, despite everything, our time here during those years was a kind of venturing.

Journal fragments, Vancouver Island

Time speeding up like the ferry, as my mother warned me it would. Adulthood passing me by, the way childhood did. But I'm beginning to see how peace of mind is possible again, and that it's time to be working towards it…

Remarkable to be sitting precisely here, daydreaming beside this particular lake, savouring the drift that can take a daydream someplace where uncertainty begins to feel like pure relief. Wonderful that we got here at last, although in a strange, circular fashion being here both distracts me from and reminds me constantly, of my son and my mother in one breath.

Not that I need reminding. It isn't effortless for us to be these holiday people. We all try to be just plain happy, and the girls are doing fine, but with Ross and me the effort shows. Grief travels with you, the happiness is bruised…

We experience this lovely island in the same unpredictable way we'll find ourselves in some other place at some other time. The fact that we're camping

at a green and lovely place called Rathtrevor Park is
a mere accident of six o'clock campground arrivals. I
am nourished by this idea of unknown moments, that
accumulation of life lying ahead, waiting, with no
possibility of existence except through the element of
accident…

Our big orange canvas tent is a nest of sleeping bags.
Kate and Nan are having too good a time for differences
of opinion, let alone squabbling. At my age they'll
remember being here, the way sitting here reminds me
of Rottnest holidays. Ross and I are aware of them
absorbing the smells of spruce and fir instead of the
eucalypts and peppermints of home, being formed
by the chill, even in summer here, of lake winds on
their skin, green winds so different from bleached sepia
and salt.

Rottnest almost always comes to mind when I think
of home. So many bridges crossed over so much water
since we were there last. Images come to mind of
sandstone and brilliant white beaches, homesickness in
their wake…

Having spent all this time in a landlocked city I'm
aware here of being surrounded by a great absence of
land. Sometimes the islands seem more like signs of that
absence than anything. Grief is so logical it's ready for
every reminder, ready to rush into any space, any shade
of blue, grey, green. Easy to imagine these islands as
rafts floating on the invisible, only broken light lapping
at them…

Along the jetty, people are standing patiently with lines taut over poised index fingers. I try to envisage the complex network below the surface.

Ross is on vacation at last; it shows in his face. He and the girls fish. Watching him cut a fish away from Nan's hook, I find the ugly truth of a creature's lip tearing as a hook is pried away from its mouth unbearable. Then watching him genuflect over dead fish and triumphant fisher-girl, it strikes me that he and I belong to the next wave moving towards that same oblivion.

See, thoughts about islands have absence and death as their underbelly. Or the ocean invokes this frame of mind, as if I should avoid the depressive tilt of the sea, although that's not it, more a matter of sights and smells breaching defences. My father would say I'm not quite there yet then, not back on track, am still *being brave*, as my mother would have put it, seeing through me...

One side of life has begun to be warm, well-tended, companionable again, even though the other side will always have its missing pieces. The grief never quite leaves, is always there to be recalled. Like being broken, you mend, but you have been altered...

Ross is a bit too deliberate still, filling gaps with the girls without realising he doesn't need to any more, compensating, at his most patient with me at times. Maybe it's a sign of healing that his gentle expecting nothing of me can be irritating sometimes, that I have moments when I would prefer him just to tell me to snap out of it. It would be a relief not to be allowed to get away with sadness any more.

Wanting to stage a command recovery must be a good thing I suppose. I do have a sense of emptying out, as if having been absorbed by grief, having absorbed it, as if we might be reaching some kind of equilibrium…

Then one afternoon we walk for miles along a beach, with Ross urging the girls to go in for a swim with him.

'You can't possibly come all this way to be near the sea and not have a swim. It would be un-Australian,' he insists.

'But it's freezing, Dad!' Nan shrieks, intrepid nevertheless, determined to be his partner in whatever he does.

Kate perches sullenly on a log further down the beach, arms folded across her chest, trailing lines in the sand with a pointed toe. She is moody, unconvinced, hates her bathers, hates herself in bathers, keeps telling me I should learn to call it a swimming costume anyway, hates the fact that I don't.

'At least learn the language, Mom,' she says.

It is no use talking to Kate in this mood – can't *imagine* where she gets it from – so I turn to the consolations of my backpack and end up reading Rilke while Ross plunges into the sea with Nan. He is bellowing, roaring.

'Holy shit! It was never like this at home!'

The word billows across the sand, how from here I now think of Calgary as home, but when I'm there, home is in Western Australia, and when we were in Fremantle, home would be Cervantes, but in Cervantes, home was Fremantle. Home: always deferred and never quite where we are. And right now more like a series of past selves than anything.

Rilke's question leaps off a page into my restless thoughts:

What is inwardness?
What if not sky intensified,
flung through with birds and deep
with winds of homecoming?

I am as entranced by such accidental relevance as by a falling star. Turning my face into the wind, grateful to be loving it, I repeat the lines to myself, memorising them while I wait for my family and whatever else it is I have this sense of waiting for: something to change, the restlessness to cease once and for all?

Thing is, it is not long since I smashed all that china – more than a mere tantrum. Much. Never again: I vow to do whatever is necessary to protect myself and everyone else from the place inside me that gave the storm shape. It is hard to see myself as that shattered woman now.

Kate's log looks like a headless, tailless whale. Impossible that such trees could ever wash up on an austere West Australian shore, so the sight seems exceptional and I take a photograph. Only Kate thinks I am taking it of her and targets me with mood as ferociously as she can from along the beach. In a minute I will go and sit with her, let her forgive me for something. It makes her feel better.

Out in the sea Nan and Ross thrash around. Watching him making his child shriek with pleasure, I feel suddenly both closer to him and more separate than I have since we met. I will not take it out on him any more, any of it. Whatever the *it* may be. I will simply love him.

Journal fragment, Vancouver Island

As if old habits of mind were always out there drifting around in the world waiting, as if the air is full of them and when you reach a certain point in a marriage, or when a marriage travels to certain places, they take possession of it despite your best efforts. As if, when we moved to Canada, they swooped and all the things we thought we'd do differently, small equalities we always just assumed, the very balance between us, began disappearing into complexities over which we were exercising too little control. Then, when the really hard things happened, I gave up...

Among the trivia of my discontent has been a tiny fact that I drove more at home because I had my own car, whereas here we share one. Here, Ross drove to work from the beginning, so drove more, so got used to the other side of the road sooner, so knew his way around more quickly, becoming used to different rules, icy roads. So Ross passed his Alberta road test while I went on clinging to renewals of an international driving permit until it was no longer legal to do so.

It is a small miracle that I found the resolve to go for the test even then, which I would not have done without Ross's coaxing and coaching. But the effect of all this is that he still takes the wheel without thinking and I head for the passenger side automatically, laziness having set in like winter.

That this should have become the state of affairs has begun to disgruntle me, a good sign. I resolve that on the return to Alberta, I will drive. I will resist feeling subjected to my husband's scrutiny and trying to drive like him, among the many complicated reasons for my capitulation. Time to get ourselves back into kilter, not least because of the messages Kate and Nan are getting from all this. I need to rebalance what I can. I am about to become that phenomenon called a landed immigrant. I expect it to feel like being released, like growing up again.

My mind taking off while I wait on the beach, I resolve to look for volunteer work, too, when we get back, to see if I can make my way into usefulness that way, decide self-indulgence is the real burden – my art, my home, my miseries, my memories, my *me*. Battling for financial equality and independence is vital, but I suspect we have lost a lot to time. Other economies, economies of the spirit, are just as important, I tell myself.

Nan's squeals recall me to sand, wind, sea. Out there fooling around with her, determined to get his family back on track, Ross is utterly appealing. We are each other's peers, I decide, no matter how the world lines us up or we line ourselves up in the world. By the time we die, we will have *lived* it together, all of it. I watch him, watch her diving from his shoulders, and for a minute or two am intent on everything that seems to mean, hoping it will be true, falling in love with my husband for the umpteenth time, and differently again.

I wander down to Kate and throw my arms around her, kissing a spot on that sweet left shoulder until she can't help herself any more and gives me a smile.

'Come on, you two!' I call eventually. 'You'll catch your deaths.'

I must stop looking for symmetry. It is not where equality lies.

Journal fragments, Vancouver Island

We've driven hundreds of miles now to *Mozart's Greatest Hits*, *Rocky Horror* and *Graceland*. We cling to Paul Simon because he reminds us of home, the irony of which doesn't escape us. But homesickness can be forced to recede in the kind of countryside we've passed through, our attention seized by mountains, desert, painted landscapes, sea-hugging roads, cathedrals of redwood and Douglas fir...

I look forward to getting back now, to doing something that counts, although it won't be teaching. Not here in Canada. It's not as if I could hope to pick up where I left off. The next set of bureaucratic obstacles will be to my Australian qualifications. Stories abound about years spent requalifying, proving, going over old ground, jumping through time-consuming hoops only to meet hurdles. They're all stories about one-upmanship and rejection, about whose credentials are superior to whose. I couldn't face it.

Not to mention lack of confidence, and I'd have little enough of that stepping back into a classroom at home after all this time. Perhaps I'm making excuses for myself, but right now I can much more easily imagine being a student and beginning all over again at something else, that process of becoming beckons...

Even now I see us leaving the island at the end of that journey, remember passing rocks striking up out of the Pacific, oversized osprey stacks, perches for a single house with a boat moored at a private jetty that pokes into the sea like a toe, enviable island homes. In the background the pert geology of Canada rears up over the city of Vancouver and forests tumble onto its beaches, beyond which this gorgeous country is perforated by lakes so clear that reflections of the sky float on them like a membrane. On our way back that year we took all this in.

I have a pho-to-graph. In fact I have many.

'First Lady of Gabriola,' Ross wrote on one of me sitting on ferry rails, sunset over the tiny island drifting past in the background, reminding us of home. Afterwards we sipped wine and talked about the seductions of islands you can never step onto, how they beckon, how passing them by can stir up a peculiar and particular melancholy.

In another picture Kate and Nan are feeding a raccoon beside the tent, with me in the background. It suggests nothing of the passion with which Ross and I were assuring them of islands at home too. I look like a much younger woman doing nothing more than sitting in a camp chair and gazing off into blue distance.

I think I was describing Rottnest to my transplanted daughters, dwelling on the charms of quokkas and trying to conjure up the Basin as a string of opal rock pools to rival any lake. Ross and I were determined to hand over blazing summer days the like of which the girls had forgotten, or never known, and sea breezes and low robust trees and subtle scrub and sand white enough to be hard on the eyes. We wanted to keep alive their birthright of the Australian mainland hovering low and mauve on the horizon like a mystery, and pods of dolphin, shipwrecks jammed onto sandstone, pied oystercatchers foraging bottoms up on reefs. Our children knew grizzly bear safety hints and the words to 'I'm Just a Sweet Transvestite', but were finding salt lakes difficult to believe in.

'What if I accidentally swallowed?'

'I like it here better.'

'Me too.'

'But why do we ever have to go back? We live here.'

'Yeah, we can stay forever now. We're immigrants.'

There we were, camping in Western Canada. Their father was taking pictures we would hardly ever look at when they were women. He was instructing his daughters about the stromatolites flowering for thousands of years in Lake Thetis's salt. I was talking about mountain duck breeding on Garden Lake and the salt-bearing winds that buffet samphire and sedge there. There was a kind of urgency to the conversations. Us, rattling on, they would say now. With the Arctic just above, so it seemed, overhearing the passing on of that legacy as carefully as happiness.

It comes rushing back that wherever there was an island I left Rottnest in the air, murmuring its name like a promise. The fact of being elsewhere illuminated everything the other island had taught me about homeland, revealing it as the place that installed my sense of leaving and looking back, a place that was part of my testimony to being alive. It was a key to my retrospections.

'At home' we would say, 'at Rotto'. Such phrases hovered in our homesick chatter, a symptom of comparisons we found ourselves making between where we were and where we came from.

Back in Calgary, I pulled out an album to show Kate and Nan a photograph of their two little heads seeming to float, disembodied and perfectly reflected on the surface of the Basin on a still hot day neither of them could have imagined by then. The wet hair plastered to their cheeks was the creamy colour of white everlastings.

Their father showed them one of the two of us walking down the beach at Geordie on our honeymoon. They shrieked at my blonde afro, so I found one of him with long hair, taken at West End. Duelling photographs. Being the photographer, Ross is the eye in our albums, has the presence of a missing person, an oversight I regret now there is so much more of life together to look back on rather than forward to, now my own hair is a version of those everlastings.

That summer on Vancouver Island I discovered our girls were growing up neither in my likeness nor their father's. They were already hybrid beings with adventurer spirits. By the time they reached their teens, they would have seen more of the world than we knew existed at their age; by the time they were women, there would be no stopping them.

By the time their mother had become *this* woman, observing her reflection in a window and piecing another phase of life together, they would have shifted into other orbits on their own behalf.

In spite of everything, we wanted Kate and Nan never to believe for a minute that love makes you dependent, must have said in a thousand ways that it should make you able to burst out of yourself, to explode out of patterns, expectations, straitjackets, able to scatter yourself in countless directions. All of which Ross has told me too when I've floundered, and I him, only he has done so much less of the floundering that the recollection arrives in his voice.

Which love has done, too, partly explaining why I should find myself so caught up now with the time my daughters spent here as children. At the present moment Kate is in Tasmania on a search for pristine wilderness to map for an eco-study. She tells me privately that she is not optimistic, there being no wildernesses left, not really, but nonetheless searches go on. In a few days Nan will arrive back in Perth from India to start work at Royal Perth Hospital, possibly on the very ward where her grandmother died.

Our daughters, off living their lives. And I – back in this slick oil city of all places – am missing them.

Journal fragments, Calgary

Being here again so unexpectedly at this stage of our lives, we endure absence like a kind of preparation, testing the indelibility of love. All of us without each other, all so far apart, like a rehearsal for our deaths...

The meanings you give to identity keep changing. Along the way I've acquired this burrow sensibility, am no longer dependent on threads connecting me to the world. Or the threads are finer, more multiple, entangle me less directly than I was capable of imagining back then. Perhaps I've tamed my desire for control, or it has tamed me...

There's a great deal to be said for crystal balls. Everything I've been pulling out of the past was shaping this unnameable future, and like all futures it's turning out to be nothing like what I expected. The problem has always been the expecting...

Sitting on that Rathtrevor beach getting my bearings all those years ago, I had no idea I would soon be driving myself to Banff, seizing a day. Or driving myself to Drumheller, that paleontological Eden nestled in the badlands and one of the world's great sites, where the bones of dinosaur herds go on being harvested and scrubbed clean with meticulous care, and where I would spend whole days in the presence of the deep past. Or any other town in Alberta, because by then I would not only know my way around, I would have the crucial identity number that allowed me to participate in the community in which I lived. I would still be singing along with ELO, a song about holding onto my dreams, to which I listened sometimes with an intensity of purpose I had last felt as a pious praying child. Or I would have turned up the radio as I drove and be singing along to Bonnie Tyler's 'Total Eclipse of the Heart'. The thing is, I would be singing.

And soon I would be spending whole days working at a women's shelter trying to teach children the consolations of art. I would be certain among other things of where in Calgary to buy better eggs, meat, coffee, books, clothes, hairstyles, children's shoes and sports gear, all because I now knew women who could tell me where to find these things. I would be connected, would even sometimes feel like a local. My accent would have become merely interesting.

Not least, I would soon have claimed the mezzanine floor in the Cascade Street house and begun my own tentative mosaic renderings, this time of my surroundings. *Treeness* at first: I remember the forms, colours and textures of trembling aspen, poplar, fir, birch, spruce. Even with the spade in my hands I knew I would not see out my days watching that tree grow, understood it would be the hardest thing to leave behind one day. So perhaps I had begun holding on through art, or letting go, or simply started taking notice of what means most to me.

Journal fragment, Calgary
In Fernie. Summer joys, poplars like green clouds,
squirrels peeling away from them like bark leaping. Ross
and I made perfect love last night, as always restored
to each other afterwards in that inexplicable way, the
chemistry going on and on. It's him, his desire finding
mine every time. He leads my inventory of blessings…

Our landed immigrant status came through quickly. The significant letter arrived looking so like any other piece of mail that I misplaced it, to Ross's horror, until Kate found it in the wrong pile on his desk. A weekend followed when we drove into the United States at Coutts, did a U-turn and re-entered Canada as immigrants.

'Welcome to Canada,' an official said. 'Congratulations.' We had landed.

'Is that all it takes?' asked my daughters.

'All there is to it,' said their father.

Six

The reality is, everyone outlives an old self, often more than one, in the course of a reasonably long life – Susan Sontag

It is difficult to see myself as that dangling, jangling woman on her blue mezzanine floor in this very city. Although I was steeping in them, our worst sorrows were behind us, a thought from which there is not much comfort to be had, since the rest lie ahead. When they arrive we will face them; there is no escaping life. That is what I was learning.

Eventually my thoughts returned to the rough and tumble of broken tiles, the cache of shattered yellow china in the basement. I first took up mosaics again by enrolling in a course, but I was dedicated by then to being a wife and mother first, my most significant change of heart. Art had become a way of rewarding myself for doing the fundamental work of our household. I had struck a bargain with my circumstances.

Journal fragments, Calgary
I catch myself having aspirations again. Kate and Nan remember little of my life back home and are not overly impressed. 'It gives you something to do at least,' they say. Not how I expected my daughters to think of me, but I begin to see that they don't need any more of me than that I be their mother. *Mom…*

In February the Bow River is a mosaic itself, a jumble of untidy textures, chunks of ice tumbling across the frozen surface ready to fall in when it melts. Someone has put a boulder out in the middle to mark the moment of the ice giving way. I see all this with an Australian eye and far down inside me have a secret impulse to slip under into the freezing flow of it, drink it, have it enter me, become a part of it, as if I could get to the source...

In this place of new beginnings there will be an exhibition. My work hangs unexpectedly beside bold images of oriental dragons, a symptom of another woman's homesickness. It turns out to be a common story, this business of art as a strategy for survival. We are a cluster of people trying not to be lost.

'Chinatown here just doesn't cut the mustard. Nor does Vancouver's,' Maggie says. 'You should see Hong Kong. Ever been to Hong Kong?' I tell her I have, remembering a night-landing between the city's glittering towers.

I buy a new dress for the occasion. 'Mom, you look absolutely gorgeous,' Katie says, adding: '*Gorgeous*: a fifteenth-century word used to describe sumptuous clothing, from Old French *gorgias* "fine, elegant", of unknown origin...' Kate is inhaling the dictionary.

The show is a success. By the end of that week I have sold work, a modest fact that makes me feel real again despite my determination to align myself with the world in more self-contained ways. Satisfaction starts working its way through me like warmth.

The blue spruce piece has displayed its red dot from the outset, being not for sale, but I decided to hang it. My heart was in it. Only, another exhibitor passing through the room pulls up and I hear him say, 'See, I told you. Bloody trees, bloody dragons, representational trash. That's what sells, every time. They bloody love it.'

I feel a rush of mortification but it passes quickly, which tells me I am making progress towards a thickening skin. On Maggie's behalf I should have asked what on earth makes our critic a believer in dragons that they might be representable at all, but the clever answers still arrive too late, and not even this swipe of derision can deflate me for long. I have accepted the sadness; it is a constant, like an organ of my body now, and I can feel other things alongside it.

A friend enthuses: 'Oh Lilith, that gold mosaic would so go with my sofa.' I resist the temptation to challenge sofa-matching; this is my work and she wants it. I am simply grateful.

These images have been making their presence felt on our mezzanine floor, in the bathroom and basement, filling my days. My fingers are sore from snipping and tweezing, and a period of intense work has been hard on my back, but I never expected to feel this plenitude again and somewhere inside me I am elated.

'The dignity of work,' I say to Ross, who is thrilled.

'I love it for you,' he says, and I feel his love. It is almost enough.

Maggie and I exchange a piece by which to remember each other.

'Representational trash,' she says, winking. 'And before you leave, I wanted to ask you, what is this thing called Chinese whispers?'

Not even the forces of irritation could deflect me. 'Mosaics, huh? Any money in it?'

'You must be so pleased not to be working these days, Lilith.'

'Lucky man, Ross – a wife who can keep herself amused...'

'How on earth do you find time for hobbies with a home to run?'

But the equivalence between time and money is drifting away. I am repossessing myself and it turns out she is no one whose existence I could have predicted.

Then, like turning a page, we were packing up the Cascade Street house to go back to Australia. The price of oil had dived and a day had arrived when another company for which Ross worked was facing disaster. Calgary, self-satisfied home of well-heeled itinerants, found itself emptying out, and we would be joining the exodus.

Journal fragment, Calgary
Around us people are speaking of the workplace as an arena, talking in terms of survival. The humiliation of colleagues seems to have been redefined as tough business practice, a sign of acumen, a win. People are being given just enough time to gather up belongings before they're escorted downstairs to the street, a process Ross tells me has been honed – yes, *honed* is the word they use – to half an hour, this after years of loyal effort sometimes. Homebuyers are handing keys back to the banks. Schools are emptying out. Apparently, an endless convoy of removal vans is heading east across the prairies...

Mosaic art requires paraphernalia. This time there is no mucking around. I bag up tiles, grout, all the bits and pieces, and put them in our bins in the alley, where neighbourhood kids will find it, garbage-picking, or from where it can go to the tip next Thursday. It seems hard to believe that by then we will be back in Perth.

Knowing better than to hang on, I have donated everything useful to shelters, art groups, friends, charities. I will ship home only the work I have made and the depleted stash of broken yellow and blue china, of which I make a bundle and bury it among my clothes.

Journal fragments, Calgary

Ross says we're travellers who stayed away too long, and for that reason leaving Calgary means leaving home again. All this packing has the feeling of waking up...

Kate talks about Cervantes a lot, which she has idealised, so it is bound to disappoint her, with its austerity, its Australian toughness, its disregard for comfort. Nan is so withdrawn Ross and I worry about what we might be doing to her. She was devastated when her bedroom furniture was sold, and when we found a new home for the goldfish she cried, certain it won't survive. Ross and I are sheltering behind efficiency, immersed in the thousand and one tasks that make a migration. They are more familiar this time, but painful, painful, as the day comes close...

A vague sense of excitement is building up behind the slurry of farewells. Time to get the girls back, I see that.

And I see white beaches, decent fish and chips, family time again. Our memories will bind us to Canada like longing, but home is coming into focus as our departure date looms – banksias, eucalypts, the smell of the sea…

The oil crash is making it seem merely sensible to leave, which helps with other prospects, like leaving friends. We all promise to stay connected, tell each other we can think of it as living in the world rather than a country, must remember we can come back, will keep in mind how the globe has shrunk. Ross and I say all this to each other too and I try to be rational, but part of me feels it should be impossible to go, as if I'm abandoning…

It was a tearing away. We would be leaving with an indelible love of mountains and prairies, four seasons, time spent. But not much consolation was to be had from reminding each other that although what must be left behind can sometimes be irreplaceable you must still leave. We all knew a blue spruce tree would go on thriving in someone else's garden.

I stand back now and examine my homemaking this time. In the windows moonlit snow falls on and on, another midnight with me gazing out at the oddly familiar and unfamiliar city of Calgary while I lose myself in thoughts of old friends, here and down at the planet's base where I have them lapped warmly by the Indian Ocean.

I had forgotten what a monochrome place this is in winter. Missing my garden at one moment, my thoughts are led through the snow to lilies, to remembering how they used to flourish in spillage from a tank tap at

Cervantes. My mother let them have the damp patch that always seemed to be there. They burst from under the tank, leaves deep green and rubbery, white velvet flowers reaching for sun, the white, white light of them. My father would mutter about noxious weeds and danger to the cattle.

'The cattle don't come anywhere near here,' she would say, so he grumbled about wasted water instead. But he only reinforced fences more carefully, laying down the law about gates more vigorously.

That waste produced perfect white blooms soaking light into life, cupping it, pooling it in the depths of their white leaflike petals. Surely it means something, cannot be worthless surely. And nothing necessarily to do with death either, I decide, reminded of the fact of their existence – Margaret, Dougal, my mother, my son – but realising that no matter what happens, no matter how significant the tearing away, there is a sameness and relentlessness to being in the world that reassures and chastens at the same time. Nothing ever really seems to change.

The feral young woman I was then is standing on a verandah in the heat. Katie is there, grizzling through her recovery from a latest bout of tonsillitis. My mother is assuring me it's just a case of having cold feet and will pass. Ross is at home waiting for my call to tell him we would or would not go to Canada with him, a call I am finding it hard to make, uncertain about going after all, but also reluctant to sabotage our grand plans. My next step would be to resign tomorrow, and it had become frightening to go ahead, which at this distance seems like a childish fork in the road, one that took us close to not living the life we are in, a loss I would regret with every cell of my being now. I remember dialling the number, as if that moment sits beside the one I am in, parallel minutes ticking along side by side.

I could grow lilies here in a pot, have their white light to myself within these glass walls, a sunny space in the daytime regardless of plunging temperatures. They could soak light into life here too, cup it, pool it in the depths of their ambiguous flowers – that single white furl of leaf-like petal, that unity which a lily seems to be.

I have been told my notions of fidelity are old fashioned fanciful nonsense, but I cling to them, believing they help love survive, let it unfurl safely from whatever kernel of passion began it. Oh, like a Moreton Bay fig, say, spreading its crown in shade patterns across a street and bearing fruit. Nothing Edenic: I have in mind a gnarled, battered, climbed-on tree on Rottnest Island, bearing graffiti some lover has knifed into its sides, a figure of all that is realistic, but great nonetheless, truly valuable and great.

Statistics have always been against us. Ross could easily have become part of all the fooling around that goes on, office girls who set their caps, as my mother used to say, at married men, all that business of men on the lookout for pert anatomy, all the professors and students, managers and secretaries, inhabitants of casting couches, the treachery of all those best friends, the dishonesty behind all that time spent away, marriages notwithstanding.

Our chances of survival would have been even worse in fiction. If this were aspiring to be 'a good story' I would have to kill Ross off. It would not be difficult. There have been close shaves. Last time we lived here, a helicopter that had just borne Ross and several colleagues back to St John's from a rig in the North Sea went down on its return flight. The shock reverberated through the industry. A friend's husband was lost with eleven others when a King Air flight crashed on its way back in the Queensland desert, caused by the plane breaking up in midair, or the pilot suffering from hypoxia, or any one of the possibilities that, for most people, stay anchored in newsprint. I remember ripples of grief. In any such story I would be left here, overwhelmed, my imagination filling with uncontainable images of Ross's last moments.

We are accustomed to uncertainty. Years ago, with *The French Lieutenant's Woman*, John Fowles contrived his famous alternative endings. In the one supposed more realistic for us, I would receive a phone call now, or someone would arrive to break the terrible news. I would never tell Ross about the begging in the streets of this complacent oil-rich city now. He would never wear the coat I bought him at Eatons because this is not cold with which you brazen it out. There would be no chance to tell him things only he would understand, like that Marta still lives in the same house – a smooth, coherent life I could never imagine – and she has invited us to dinner when he gets back. I could not tell him how nervous the prospect makes me, how afraid I am of sadness that might stir even now, but how I look forward to seeing our old garden, the private heart of our return. I would never tell him Marta lost track of Colleen, heard a rumour that she remarried and moved to New Zealand, but doesn't know her surname. Some of us passed in and out of each other's lives like flickers of fish.

Perhaps such a story should take us home instead and have us avoid growing old by curling up together to shuffle off our particular mortal coil entwined in some leisurely pact – we have all heard of them and even secretly admire them under certain circumstances. Or we could have gone up the Trade Center towers that day instead of when we did, so our story would hitch itself to tragedy like a parasite. Or I discover I have only weeks to live and we detour into the sad disentanglement people face every day as they become preoccupied with the prospect of their own death. Or we could have been in any one of a number of planes, cars, ferries, Ferris wheels at any number of wrong times. Any of these can happen yet, still will, since something must, so they hover on our story's fringes, fill its shadows and silences with the inevitable.

In any event, Ross and I are way beyond slick romance and have been together far too long for anyone to mourn the tragedy of a passion presumed wasted, but I contend that what would be lost instead is possibly something greater, deeper, the incalculable ordinariness of which cannot be explained and remains in progress for as long as we live. The stories don't say anything about this.

Since this is neither fact nor fiction, however, or since it is both, I am off the hook. In a tilt at the story after the story ends, I can choose the most likely ending, that we will live out the rest of our lives in the *happily*, since *ever after* has never applied to biological beings. In reality Ross and I will probably end our days together with one of us bundled up in rugs, the other watching the fading-away, possibly at such length that all the vitality of life spent living together seems like a deep apparition we can only dip our memory into, if we still have one. One way or another, one of us must disappear, possibly through a wall of pain, and the other will have no choice but to improvise the rest.

When Ross gets back and I emerge from this snow-aquarium in which I have been drifting wutheringly about, I will kiss him and he will kiss me. His lips will be warm and full. There will be aeroplane smells in his clothes. We'll sleep first and only after that make love, because that is how it is these days and we have all the time in the world.

Over breakfast, which he will cook, we will swap stories, fill out each other's worlds again. We'll go for a walk, ring our daughters the minute time zones meet, soon visit an old friend we have not seen for a very long time, find ourselves walking past a house where we had another child many years ago, a house that must have our grief in its very pores — but even that I am prepared to meet again. Step by step, we'll keep improvising our way across this happily-ever-after that ought to be among the stories worth telling and is not told enough, perhaps because a marriage (like a tango) has to be danced step by step to the end.

Journal fragments, Calgary

Nothing at all has arrived from the girls for my birthday. I suppose a call will come, or their greetings will be somewhere in the ether. These international moves still entail a complicated communication chain. I hope it isn't a sign of us getting used to each other's absences. I try

to imagine one of them arriving, a knock at the door –
Surpri-ise! – but it's unimaginable…

I have become one, single, an isolate. Everything I've
ever done and been is behind me. Today I am as old as
my mother was when she died. I can feel the edges of
my own existence…

So I take myself out to dinner. Gloved, scarved, swaddled
in a thick green overcoat that makes me invulnerable to
the cold, lost in thought, I feel a sense of self-sufficiency
wash over me. It is as invigorating as the river air when I
push open the door to Georgiana's café and am enveloped
in warmth.

Over a lamb curry I watch people, especially a couple
sitting in the window, but not many are out in this weather
and soon I am the only person there. I remember a meal
Ross and I had the night before he left, at a pasta joint
where it was hard to talk over the noise from the next
table, so we ate pretty much in sluggish silence. We *were*
sluggish. When you move a sea-level body to the high
prairies and into dry mountain winter air you must be
prepared to feel debilitated. Ross and I had forgotten what
Calgary winters are like, how the air sucks moisture out
of you.

'It can take a full year for the body to adapt,' the doctor
said.

I don't recall it taking so long last time, but we were
younger, are learning more every year about the body
having a mind of its own. The last weeks at home had
been tiring and unsettling, and that night I felt like some

docile marine creature dropping into the depths until a storm had subsided. Then a conversation next to us took over the space.

'Fifty-five,' a young man yelled.

'No, fifty.' There was a shriek of laughter.

'Yeah, fifty's well and truly past it.'

'At our office they just promoted a woman who's gotta be at least that.'

'We've been getting rid of them at our place.'

'We're working on it.'

'Oh you guys! Come on, forty-five.'

'Jeez, that's only ten years away.'

'Yeah, but you're old.'

Their boozy laughter filled the room and bids went back and forth about cut-off points and closed books. Ross and I watched the fake fire and could only listen, had no choice, were rendered invisible. Tonight I only pity the baby couples who buy the disillusionment story and think life will be over so soon. Did we tell it too, before we were lucky enough to know better, when we thought we would be young and cocky forever? My mind wanders to another noisy table, at a restaurant in Fremantle, the two of us kissing tartufo kisses.

And now this.

Of all things, a sulphur-crested cockatoo is roaming the room and I wonder by what complicated route my feathered compatriot comes to be perched on the back of a chair in so unsuitable a place. It blinks and chews a toy motorcycle and seems pleased to be spoken to. I fancy it recognises my accent. Its mistress certainly does. It turns out Georgiana is South African, but has settled here.

I envy the certainty in her voice.

'Oh yes, I'm here absolutely for good,' she says.

At Customs and Immigration this time I handed officialdom a passport in which my photograph is six years out of date. With my hair still red and shoulder-length I look nothing like my present self, but no one seemed to care. Tucked into it, on the little green form against 'occupation', I had scrawled the word *wife*. No hesitation over the label this time, because I could just as easily have written housewife, companion, artist, teacher, mother, home duties, tiler, painter, bold-faced jig. I can never predict how I will fill in that impertinent, reductive, often nullifying little space. To my mind, what word I write only exemplifies the meaninglessness of little green forms, except as exercises in cooperation and camouflage. The word *wife*, this time, suited my mood.

Now I am old enough to know that what may appear dull to the uninitiated is often a fine patina of love over life. What matters is the two of you, how long things last.

I confide to Georgiana that it is my birthday. As if age were a country of origin, I recognise everything about her: a tie-dyed sarong, the music of Santana playing in the background, the walls covered with her own delicate signed sketches of Persian architecture and veiled women, the ceiling strung with philodendron vines. The café is pure 1970s, a cauldron of remembered pleasures now called *retro*. Talking with her about the bird, birthdays, migration, Australia, art, I feel restored. Everything I could ever pull out of the past was shaping this moment and, like all futures, this grungy little café in Calgary is not what I expected.

This time tomorrow Ross should be telling me tales of Newfoundland and offshore oil rigs and storms in the North Atlantic. I hope so fervently as I pay the bill, self-consciously slow because my bad hand misbehaves in the cold and the unfamiliar currency demands attention. I'll bring him to Georgiana's for a chicken curry, I decide, redo a birthday dinner with him. He will love the place.

On my way back to the apartment the crunch of snow underfoot catches at me like discordant music. I look up at our building. Snowflakes will spin down and bounce off that sill fifteen floors above the street all night, swirling off into the flurry the way they are now. Inside, the apartment is warm and pinkly illuminated by high-rise lights. The living room embraces me like a home for the first time. I sit in the window with a cup of coffee, watching steam billow above buildings as Calgary tries desperately to heat itself.

Journal fragment, Calgary

She is out there floating like a ghost again, falling snow whitening her hair. When I move, she moves. I bare my teeth and she grimaces with the cold. I touch my face and it looks as if her hand is scratching at the glass to get in. The illusion depresses me. A day can be such a long time…

Of course the remedy would be to get up from the desk. Then she will be back inside and the window will turn out to have been full of nothing more than light on snow. But I only have to sit here again and she will be back out there, copying my every move, smiling at me when I smile, deepening the lines on my face into creases. There is nothing friendly in the reflection.

Facts must be faced, so before going to bed I tear packing tape from the lips of another carton. Shoes fall out with Ross's laces caught up in mine as they tumble into the room, shoes we wore through Europe so they remind me of France.

Straightening up, I catch sight of myself with my arms full, a familiar pose. Usually, I would be holding a pillowcase heavy with tiles, china or glass, away from myself, as if the bag contained a cobra – I always half-expect splinters to escape and cost me my eyes, a particular fear as if other wounds can be relied upon to heal. I should wear safety glasses, but they make me feel like a fish bumping up against glass where I expect open water. So instead I hold the pillowcase away from me and turn my head aside while I take to it with a hammer.

Seeing my reflection, it occurs to me that I love the sound of that shattering, full of possibility and promise, a beginning. The next step is accidental and random, a moment when shapes and mixtures of colour seem given, as if something is anterior to the process and I catch a whiff of its presence when I empty out those first broken pieces. After that comes work, the kind of work that feels like a deliberate elaboration of self. But before, in the smashing and revealing of first possibilities, something seems almost divine. In this fashion I have found along the way that there's more to mosaics than meets the eye – somewhere, something: connections, fusions, confusions, patterns of thought.

A mosaicist does not traffic in seamlessness. Wildly textured surfaces and grout lines throwing shape at the eye are all part of the deal. Images bloom out of colour itself. It is a medium in which everything seems to happen at once.

Having put away the several pairs of shoes and added another box to the dismantled stack, I avoid silence by putting on some music before going to bed: Leonard Cohen, *The Future* for me, Midnight Oil for Ross, in case he does come back tonight. All part of the effort of feeling at home here. Then, hoping to be asleep before it finishes, I lie in the dark trying to imagine what he could be doing at precisely this minute.

Such speculations are easy. He has drawn diagrams of the rig, the supply boat lunging skyward as it manoeuvres in a heavy sea. A diagram can only go so far, but is better than nothing in the process of sharing a life.

He tells wonderful stories about being on rigs, like waking up on the Grand Banks to hear someone yelling, 'Well, how in Christ's name did it get there?' and going down to see a piece of iceberg blundering between the caissons.

'They call it a bit. A bergie bit. They break away and this one must have been just small enough to duck under the deck in a trough. It would have needed perfect timing: normally they'd push off under their own weight and float away. It was about the size of the rocks off Cervantes,' he explained, 'only smoother. And imagine it glacial blue.'

Not an easy comparison, but his suggestion gives me perspective on its size and adds unearthly beauty to my visions of trapped dwarf icebergs now. I see tiny islands, a chipped continent; the blue in my mind's eye is a turquoise Indian Ocean shading into transparency at the shore.

'How did you get to be so cool about storms in the middle of the North Atlantic?' I asked him. 'And icebergs off Newfoundland?' Such conversations usually mean he has been away, or is leaving.

'How on earth did we end up back here?' I said before he left this time. It was a rhetorical question.

'Who says we've ended up?' he replied nevertheless.

I remember a photograph he once emailed me, of an iceberg billowing below the surface, an inverted explosion of ice, a flowering of blue immensity into the ocean's depths. Such gifts have given my life more layers. We see behind each other, are the eyes in the back of each other's head, fill out each other's view of the world, two heads being better than one.

The world I bring him may be smaller, but the glow of light on porcelain scraps has its place. I may read Rilke and dream of a moonlit window seat, say, try to dismantle it in my imagination, wonder how I might render it – in what, silver-grouted alabaster chips, white porcelain tesserae? – and meanwhile Ross photographs the world, its textures, tells true stories in light, is able to take a picture of the moon in which its light lies down on paper for him. He is provider *and* artist.

Not that I am a failed dreamer. After all, everything depends on the scale of the dreams and mine, being dreams of true love and constant flight, have a certain grandeur. I fly regularly in my sleep, alighting here and there, walking once on the surface of the ocean for hours, and once among peach trees in full blossom, through which the dream seemed to be telling me I would be drifting for the rest of my life. I have collected: photographs, seeds, stones, shells, bones, skeletons, quotations, things that have helped me live with myself. Such are the keepsakes.

The truth of the matter – that I will never pass this way again and in a couple of generations no one will remember I passed this way at all – is becoming as comfortable as an old T-shirt. My present-tense hair is grey and brisk. I can face other facts, too: like that Ross and I, having loved each other well, are still at it; like that true love is real, only the trick is recognising it when you see it.

Or it is the luck of the draw? I am not smug; luck *is*. Powerful chemistry is still getting us through the transformations. Remembering Ross's experience just before we left home, I decide love can be as precarious as walking over all those beetles: you feel all the small deaths underfoot. The beetle can't predict its death. It assumes its own survival until the crunch comes. We have been lucky in love. The end will simply arrive.

When he gets home we'll go for a walk along the river – after sitting in a plane all day he'll want fresh air and exercise. I have at least bent over, stood up, lifted, stored, arranged, sorted, and today walked to and from Kensington. Here, in my bed, with the sound of Leonard Cohen drifting down the hall, rollicking words about closing time, I think I should count my blessings.

I remember reading somewhere that *blessing* translates into Hebrew as *more life*, which is all I am sure about, that I want more, more, more.

Like every other night, I do eventually sleep.

The Atlantic rushes the legs of the semi-submersible. The structure wants to roll with every wave, strains against its anchors. The supply boat surfs trough after trough less than a kilometre away, but in the dark the only sign of its presence is an occasional flicker of light. The chains clank inside the caissons as swells come through. The storm has been forecast to hit at about nine – waves could be a hundred feet – and the rig is ready for it.

Ross stands on the lower deck looking down into light that floods the surface of the moon pool. He is grateful for the freezing night air. For the first thirty-six hours here he was violently sick, until the doctor finally admitted his sea legs weren't kicking in and gave him a shot. It worked, but he hasn't spent a single minute feeling well since. He breathes in, hard.

Waves pull at the rig and it tugs against the seabed. He thinks back to the Ocean Ranger. They got off, but their lifeboats broke up against the side of the standby vessel. Eighty-four men died. Out here, such disasters become imaginable, but he's relieved to be here nevertheless, so far from office-bound.

Four puffins swim into the moon pool to fish under the lights, tiny but unperturbed by the violence foaming around them, or the depths under them, or the massive darkness surrounding the field of light, into which they disappear at times only to re-emerge with the next wave. A whole ocean is trying to swallow them; their bones ought not to be able to withstand the force. Ross searches for words – they frolic, seem impervious to danger, their antics are a kind of nose-thumbing at the awesome power of such a sea.

It is hard to believe only a month has passed since he and Lilith were standing beside each other at Rottnest watching seals do much the same thing. They'd come in for shelter there too, only that time he was the one fishing, until they arrived that is. And he didn't have floodlights bringing fish to the surface like this. Most of his fishing memories are fishless – a rare moment of self-pity. Then there was the afternoon they stood on the jetty at Cervantes watching dolphins. Now this.

He looks up. The stars are invisible. It is a black, black night. He misses Lilith, and the girls seem abysmally far away and too much time has passed since he last saw them. If it weren't for the puffins, he'd feel alone in the universe, a weird feeling that makes him feel large and small at the same time. The sublime, he remembers. Lilith has a taste for it. *She'd love this*, he thinks.

I am still awake when the doorbell rings. Musing about *pique assiette* mosaics, as it happens, how the label derives from a pretty word meaning someone who eats off another's plate. I am reaching the conclusion that this describes my situation exactly, that I am *picassiette* personified, when I hear it ring. Security would never let anyone else up here without calling ahead, especially at this time of night, so unless it *is* security, of course it must be Ross and of course he must have forgotten his key.

The bed looks different, suddenly. I remove the tossed books, my cardigan, put his pillow back where it belongs. A coffee stain is visible on my bathrobe, so there is no need to switch on lights, this city room is never dark.

My steps are muffled in the corridor and it crosses my mind that you can almost tell from the sound that the carpet is beige. The air is so dry I am building up static electricity, know I should touch something else before I touch Ross – kisses in this place can be highly charged, the spark visible in the dark. In the end this is all there will ever be to it, an accumulation of footsteps, because, in the end, only the present tense ever really is.

ACKNOWLEDGEMENTS

This is a work of fiction. Liberties have been taken. Cervantes undoubtedly bears only the most superficial resemblance to the real town in Western Australia, and this version of Calgary is the retrospective impression of an affectionate visitor.

I am indebted to friends and family whose experiences lodged in my imagination over decades of shared history, often supporting the notion of memory as a collective enterprise. Specifically, to Leo Killigrew I owe the story of spiders on a moonlit lake, and to Gibb Macdonald the bitter observation that an obstetrician must have heard a ghost.

My thanks to Karen Sparnon, author of *Madonna of the Eucalypts* (Text, 2006), for her encouragement not only in awarding first prize to an earlier version of this work in the 2008 Ellen Gudrun Kastan Literary Award, but for her reviving interest afterwards. It made a difference. As has the much appreciated writerly companionship of Karen Throssell, John Jenkins, Catherine Hainstock, Anne Connor and Cheryl Simpson.

I am very grateful to everyone at UWA Publishing: Terri-ann White for her warm reception of the manuscript, Kate Pickard for reassuring guidance, Linda Martin for a generous beginning. My thanks to Jon MacDonald at XOU Design for the perfect cover image. I am especially indebted to Nicola Young for giving these pages her scrupulous literary attention, for the refinements of her editorial eye, for scientific facts, for insightful questions.

Benjamin and Cassandra Macdonald are at the heart of the matter in ways that go without saying and I thank them.

As I do Jane Southwell, Lekkie Hopkins, Susan Midalia and Pamela Bagworth for their treasured creative friendship and literary erudition throughout the staccato process of writing. In particular, I thank Susan Midalia for her immeasurable support and editorial gifts. Without her this novella would not have been published.

Without David Macdonald it would not have been written.

PERMISSIONS

SOURCES

Atwood, Margaret, 'Two Dreams', *Morning in the Burned House*, McLelland & Stewart, Toronto, 1995, pp. 96–7.

Barth, John, *On with the Story*, Little, Brown and Company, Boston, 1996, p. 50.

Carson, Anne, *The Beauty of the Husband: A Fictional Essay in 29 Tangos*, New York: Alfred A. Knopf, New York, 2001, p. 21. (Carson cites the quotation from John Keats as a note on Keats' copy of *Paradise Lost*, I.)

Chekhov, Anton, 'Heartache', 1886, from *The Portable Chekhov*, ed. and trans. Avrahm Yarmolinsky, Penguin Group (USA) Inc., New York, 1947, p. 123.

Dillard, Annie, *Pilgrim at Tinker Creek*, Harper Collins, New York, 1985, p. 84.

Fischer, Peter, *Mosaic: History and Technique*, Thames & Hudson, London, 1971, pp. 7–8.

Kierkegaard, Søren, 'Works of Love,' trans. Lillian Marvin Swenson, in *A Kierkegaard Anthology*, ed. Robert Bretall, Princeton University Press, Princeton, New Jersey, 1946, p. 296.

Kincaid, Jamaica, *At the Bottom of the River*, Farrar Strauss Giroux, New York, 1983, p. 69.

Malcolm, Janet, *Regarding Chekhov: A Critical Journey*, Random

House, New York & Toronto, 2001, pp. 15–16. (Here Malcolm describes Chekhov's antipathy for self-description.)

Rilke, Rainer Maria, 'Paris, Summer before July 6th,' trans. Edward Snow, in *Uncollected Poems*, Farrar, Straus & Giroux, North Point Press, New York, 1996, p. 595.

Roberts, Michèle, *The Looking Glass*, Little, Brown and Company, London, 2000, p. 237.

Sontag, Susan, *Where the Stress Falls*, Random House, London, 2002, p. 56.

Wordsworth, William, 'A slumber did my spirit seal,' *Lyrical Ballads*, vol. II, 1799, in John Butt (ed.), *Wordsworth: Selected Poetry and Prose*, Oxford University Press, 1964, p. 136. (This is the source of the quote 'rolled round in earth's diurnal course' on page 95.)

Carmel Macdonald Grahame has published short fiction, poetry, critical essays and reviews in journals, periodicals and anthologies here and in North America. She has a PhD in Australian literature, and for several years taught courses in literature and creative writing at secondary and tertiary levels in her home state of Western Australia. She lives in Warrandyte, Victoria.

Printed in Australia
AUOC02n1035260314
260388AU00001B/1/P